"Brock? Do you have a minute?"

Elana's voice made Brock stop and turn in amazement. She'd called out to him. Voluntarily. Her dark eyes were warm and welcoming, making her even more beautiful than the first time he'd seen her at work. "Elana. It's great to see you."

Her tremulous smile made his chest tighten with anticipation. "I've been looking all over for you, Brock. I wanted to say I'm sorry. I'm so sorry for the way I treated you the other day. I had no right to be angry with you."

"I—don't know what to say. Does this mean you've forgiven me?" He could barely allow himself to hope.

She smiled. "Yes, Brock. I forgive you."

The incessant ringing of his phone pulled him from the dream. With a low groan of regret, Brock pried his eyes open.

Dear Reader

Many of us have done things in our past that we regret. Unfortunately there is no way to go back and fix the mistakes we've made, so somehow we end up finding a way to live with them.

But what if the mistake is something that has far-reaching consequences? Life and death consequences? This is the main dilemma facing Elana and Brock in their touching story of love and forgiveness.

Brock Madison was driving his car when Elana's sister pulled out in front of him. The crash wasn't his fault, but Elana's sister died at the scene despite his efforts to save her. Nine years later, Elana finds herself working for Brock at Trinity Medical Center's Emergency Department. They are both dedicated to their careers, but will they let go of the pain from the past in order to find love and happiness?

I hope you enjoy THE NURSE'S BROODING BOSS. I love to hear from my readers, so please stop by and visit me at www.lauraiding.com

Happy Reading!

Laura

THE NURSE'S
BROODING BOSS

BY
LAURA IDING

First published in Great Britain 2010
Harlequin Mills & Boon Limited,
Eton House, 18-24 Paradise Road, Richmond, Surrey TW9 1SR

© Laura Iding 2010

ISBN: 978 0 263 21491 8

Laura Iding loved reading as a child, and when she ran out of books she readily made up her own, completing a little detective mini-series when she was twelve. But, despite her aspirations for being an author, her parents insisted she look into a 'real' career. So the summer after she turned thirteen she volunteered as a Candy Striper, and fell in love with nursing. Now, after twenty years of experience in trauma/critical care, she's thrilled to combine her career and her hobby into one—writing Medical™ Romances for Mills & Boon®. Laura lives in the northern part of the United States, and spends all her spare time with her two teenage kids (help!)—a daughter and a son—and her husband. Enjoy!

Recent titles by the same author:

THE SURGEON'S NEW-YEAR WEDDING WISH*
EXPECTING A CHRISTMAS MIRACLE*
MARRYING THE PLAYBOY DOCTOR*
EMERGENCY: SINGLE DAD, MOTHER NEEDED

Cedar Bluff Hospital trilogy

To the wonderful, wild, wacky women of CAFA.
I look forward to seeing you every year.

CHAPTER ONE

ELANA SCHULTZ dashed into the emergency department of Trinity Medical Center, heading straight for the time clock, swiping her badge at exactly three o'clock in the afternoon.

On time. Barely. Breathing a sigh of relief that she'd made it, she quickly stuffed her purse into her staff locker and crossed over to the arena where the charge nurse was going through the shift assignments.

"Elana, you and Raine will take the trauma bay," Stacey informed them. "Suzette, you're taking the urgent care area. Emma, you're arena team one. Liz, you're arena team two…"

"How was your long weekend?" Raine asked in a hushed whisper so as not to interrupt Stacey's monologue.

"Good. Everything went well. I'll fill you in later," Elana whispered back.

"Any questions about the assignments?" Stacey asked, looking up from her clipboard. After a moment of silence she nodded. "All right, there are twenty-seven patients on the board, with eleven still waiting to be seen. The trauma bay is currently empty; the last patient has been dispatched to the medical ICU. It's been a busy day, but not too crazy. Let's hope it stays that way for our shift." Stacey set her clipboard aside. "Call me if you need help."

That was their cue to leave. The group of nurses broke up, scattering to their various assignments.

"How's your aunt Chloe?" Raine asked as she fell into step beside Elana on their way to the trauma bay.

"She's much better. Her cardiac stent procedure went off without a hitch." Technically, Chloe Jenkins wasn't Elana's blood relative, she was Elana's foster mother, the last and by far the best in a string of horrible experiences. If not for Chloe, Elana knew there was a very good chance she would have ended up on the streets.

She owed Chloe her life.

"I'm so glad she's doing all right," Raine said softly.

Elana smiled. "Me too. You know how close I am to Chloe." Her mother, Louisa Schultz, had been in a nursing home since Elana was fifteen after suffering a complete relapse of her nervous breakdown. Her mother's emotional state had collapsed after Elana's father had walked out on them. She'd gotten better slowly over time until Felicity's death had sent her into a deep emotional breakdown. Elana still loved her mother and faithfully visited every weekend, but it had been nine years, and her mother still hadn't spoken a single word.

"You missed the big announcement while you were gone," Raine said.

Elana raised a brow and took the trauma pager from

the first shift trauma nurse, who looked all too eager to give it up. "What? We're all getting pay raises?"

"Yeah, right." Raine let out a snort of laughter. "No. There's a new doctor on staff. He started the day after you left, as a matter of fact."

Elana shrugged, sweeping a gaze over the trauma bay. She got along fine with the doctors she worked with, but she didn't go ga-ga over them like some of the other nurses did. Most of the doctors were married anyway, and the ones who weren't were—in her opinion— single for a reason.

"I'm telling you, Elana, he's hot. And he's single. At least, I'm pretty sure he is—Suzette was pumping him for personal information."

Their trauma pagers went off simultaneously, interrupting Raine's story. Elana read the text message.

Motor vehicle crash, 23 y/o female trauma victim ejected from the car, intubated on the scene. ETA two minutes.

Motor vehicle crash. Female trauma victim ejected from the car. Just like Felicity had been.

Elana swallowed hard and clipped her pager back onto the waistband of her scrub pants. Even after nine years, any reminder about her sister's tragic death made her feel sad. With her mother's emotional collapse and her absent father, Elana's life had spiraled downhill. Thank heavens for Chloe, who'd rescued her before she was too far gone.

"I wonder if he's working today?" Raine asked.

It took her a minute to figure out Raine was still talking about the new doctor.

"How do you know he's single?" Elana asked.

"Because Suzette talked to him. Weren't you listening? He's young, just turned thirty, and he's hot. Like, steamy hot."

No, she hadn't been listening. Elana shrugged again and crossed over to the supply cabinet, opening drawers and ensuring the day shift staff had restocked everything after the last trauma patient had been transferred up to the medical ICU.

"There he is," Raine hissed.

Before she could turn to look, the double doors of the ambulance bay burst open. Two paramedics wheeled in the young female trauma patient. Elana took her place at the right side of the patient, while Raine took the left. Trauma resuscitations were not as chaotic as they were made to look on television. Every person had their role to play, and predesignated responsibilities, depending on where they stood. Elana tended to take the right side because she liked doing the vital signs and initial assessment.

"Two liters of Ringer's lactate are going into respective antecubital eighteen-gauge IVs. Suspected cervical fracture, limbs flaccid at the scene, C-collar in place. Intubated in the field with a seven-point-five endotracheal tube."

Elana connected the patient to the heart monitor, listening as the paramedics rattled off the pertinent information. The new doctor stood at the foot of the bed, but Elana's attention was riveted on the patient. This young woman was older than Felicity had been, but only by a couple of years.

A suspected cervical fracture. Possibly paralyzed for life. How awful. Felicity had died at the scene of her accident, but, really, which fate was worse? Staring down at the young woman's blood-streaked face, Elana wasn't sure.

She did a quick assessment, getting the first set of vital signs and doing a quick listen to the patient's heart and lungs. When she finished, she flipped her stethoscope around her neck. "Vitals are low, BP 76/40, pulse tachy at 122, pupils sluggish but reactive and equal in size. Lungs coarse but bilateral breath sounds noted." She glanced up at the new physician and froze.

Brock Madison.

Her chest tightened, and she had to remind herself to breathe. No, it couldn't be. She had to be mistaken. She hadn't seen him in years. Maybe this guy just looked like an older version of the Brock Madison she remembered.

"Do you want to continue the Ringer's lactate solution, Dr Madison?" Raine asked.

"Yes, although we may need to transfuse a unit of blood too."

The room spun, and Elana had to grab onto the side rail to keep herself upright. Dr Madison. Brock Madison was the new doctor on staff.

And he was also the driver of the car that had hit her sister's vehicle nine years ago. The man who'd caused Felicity's death.

* * *

Brock hid his surprise at seeing Elana Schultz again, although the shocked expression on her face mirrored the turmoil in his gut. With an effort, he forced himself to ignore his personal problems and concentrate on the young trauma victim before him.

"Start with two units of O-negative blood," Brock ordered. "We need to get her stabilized before we send her to the CT scanner to evaluate the extent of her injuries."

Raine did as he asked, but Elana simply stood there, hanging onto the side rail and staring down at the patient, clearly in shock. As much as he appreciated what she must be going through, at this critical juncture he needed the entire trauma team to be working together. He moved closer, keeping his voice low so it wouldn't carry. "Elana, if you can't do this, please find someone to take your place."

She snapped her head around to look at him. The fierce expression flaring in her eyes nearly made him take a step backward. After a moment's hesitation, she glanced away, took a deep breath and let it out slowly, unclasping her tense fingers from the side rail. "I'm fine. Do you want a full set of labs?"

"Yes. We need to know if she's bleeding internally." Brock couldn't help admiring the way Elana jumped back into the trauma resuscitation. He'd known she'd graduated from college with a nursing degree because he'd kept tabs on Felicity's younger sister over the years. But he hadn't realized Elana had taken a position here at Trinity. Ironic that she'd chosen to work in the emergency department, providing care to trauma patients. Like her sister.

And yet hadn't he gone into emergency medicine for the same reasons?

He watched as she drew a set of blood gases and then filled another four lab tubes with blood. Reassured that Elana was doing all right, he turned his attention back to the patient. He was somewhat worried about the young woman's lung function, but, even more, he needed to know what her hematocrit and hemoglobin levels were.

"Get me those H & H results stat. In the meantime, let's make sure there are no other obvious sites of bleeding."

Elana and Raine worked well together, he noted. Since arriving at Trinity Medical Center, he'd been impressed with how well the emergency and trauma center staff gelled, from the techs to the nurses up to and including the physicians. A true team approach. Things hadn't been quite this cohesive in his former position.

Within a few minutes, Elana reported new vitals. "BP up to 84/42, pulse a little less tachy at 117. We're making some headway."

He nodded, agreeing with her assessment. If they could get this patient's blood pressure up to the nineties, he'd be satisfied enough to send her to the CT scanner. If she needed emergency surgery on her spine, he didn't want to delay care. On the other hand, he didn't want her to crash in the CT scanner, either.

"We have the H & H results," Elana announced. "Hemoglobin is 7.8 and hematocrit is 29."

"Give another two units of O-negative blood, Raine," he ordered. "Keep running the fluids too; I'd like to see her systolic blood pressure over ninety. I'm going to call Radiology to make sure they're ready for her. One of you is going to need to go with her to the CT scanner."

"I'll go," Elana volunteered.

He gave a brief nod, turned on his heel and walked to the nearest phone. Within moments he had everything arranged with the radiologist on call.

His gaze settled back on Elana, watching her as she worked. With her jet-black hair pulled into a long pony-tail, her high cheekbones and olive-toned skin, a gift from her Hispanic mother, she was stunningly beautiful. She'd grown up from the gangly teenager she'd been nine years ago.

And she had every reason to hate him.

The familiar guilt surged like bile in the back of his throat. He tore his gaze away and swallowed hard, trying to focus on the monitor above the female trauma patient's head. This wasn't the time or the place to wallow in the mistakes of the past.

"Blood pressure is up to 95 systolic after the first unit of blood. We still have one more unit to give, but she seems to have stabilized for now. Do you want me to take her for a CT scan?" Elana asked.

He nodded, the lump lodged in the back of his throat making it impossible to speak.

She didn't need to be asked twice. Within moments, she and Raine had the patient disconnected from the main monitor and reconnected to the portable one they used for transporting patients. As Elana whisked the patient away, he found himself wondering if she'd volunteered to go to the CT scan for the sole purpose of getting away from him.

Possibly. No, probably. Damn. The last thing he wanted to do was to cause Elana any more grief. He certainly didn't want her to quit her job because of him. She must love trauma nursing to have chosen to work here, and Trinity Medical Center was the only level-one trauma center in Southeastern Wisconsin.

He sighed and scrubbed his hand over his face. Talk about his rotten timing. If he'd known Elana was working here, he could have handled their first meeting a little differently.

No, who was he trying to kid? There was nothing he could have done to make this meeting easier for her. The scalding look she'd sent him had stabbed deep. He'd leave himself if not for the fact that his brother needed him. And the fact that he'd signed a twelve-month contract.

"So, Dr Madison, how do you like it here at Trinity so far?" Raine asked, cleaning up the area around the trauma bay.

He cleared his throat. "It's great. I'm glad I made the move from Minneapolis."

"Minneapolis's loss is our gain," Raine said with a smile.

Raine was pretty enough with her dark red hair and her bright green eyes, but he wasn't interested in the signals she was sending out. He didn't date, especially anyone who might be interested in a future. He couldn't help glancing at his watch, wondering where Elana was.

He wished they could talk. There had to be some way to ease the tension that shimmered between them.

For years he'd longed for a chance to explain. To redeem himself in her eyes if at all possible.

So much for seeking forgiveness. Remembering the banked fury in her dark eyes, he knew there was no chance in hell Elana would give him that option.

He didn't deserve her forgiveness.

"How much longer?" Elana asked, casting a worried glance at her patient. The young patient's name was Jamie Edgar, and her blood pressure was starting to slip downward.

"Ten minutes," the tech assured her.

She increased the flow of the fluids to help maintain Jamie's blood pressure. Keeping busy was helping her to forget about Brock Madison, who happened to be waiting for them in the trauma bay.

What on earth had she done to deserve this? Why after all these years was it her misfortune to have to work with the man she despised?

She rubbed her aching temple, hearing Chloe admonishing her in her mind. *Don't talk like that, young lady. Brock Madison wasn't the person at fault in the accident, your sister was. She pulled out right in front of him! It's certainly not his fault Felicity died.*

In some tiny corner of her mind Elana knew Chloe was right. Her sister had pulled out onto the busy highway in front of Brock without warning. But he'd also been speeding, at least according to one of the witnesses on the scene. Brock's father had been a cop at the time, and everyone thought his dad had pulled strings to cover up the truth.

Including Elana.

Besides, did it matter? The irrevocable fact remained that Brock stole Felicity's life.

Nothing on earth could change that.

And now she'd be forced to work with the man she detested.

"There, we're all finished." The radiology tech broke into her troubled thoughts. "Do you want me to call the ED to let them know you're on your way back?"

She forced a smile. "Sure, that would be great."

Jamie's blood pressure slipped a little further, and Elana quickened her pace, pushing the gurney as fast as she dared, keeping one eye on the monitor and the other on the hallway. Luckily, the radiology department was not far from the emergency department.

"I'm losing her blood pressure," Elana announced as she entered the trauma bay.

"Hang another unit of O-neg blood. The spine surgeons are on their way down. The radiologist already called me with the CT results. She has a severe compression fracture in her cervical spine. If they can operate quickly, they might be able to minimize the damage to the spinal cord."

Elana nodded, indicating she'd heard him. Relieved that the spine damage may not be permanent, she made sure Jamie was ready for the OR, taking off her rings and her necklace and putting them into a valuables envelope to be stored in the hospital safe.

The OR team showed up and took over the case, taking Jamie straight up to surgery. Once her patient was gone, Elana felt the all too familiar letdown. She enjoyed trauma nursing, but there was a part of her that had considered moving to the critical care area so that she could follow the trauma cases more closely. She'd miss the thrill of caring for patients coming in right from the scene, but it would also be great to see some of these patients actually recover.

"Elana? Are you all right?"

She glanced at Brock, her stomach knotting with apprehension. How could she be all right with him around? She needed to get away from him. Far, far away. "Of course. Excuse me while I restock the supplies before the next trauma call comes in."

"I'll do it," Raine offered, glancing between Elana and Brock with frank curiosity.

She ground her teeth together, wishing Raine wouldn't try to be quite so helpful. Since Raine hurried to do the stocking, and Brock simply stood there, watching her with concern, she turned and headed towards the staff lounge. Unfortunately she wasn't going to get the privacy she needed since Brock was right behind her.

"What do you want?" she asked, spinning around to face him and crossing her arms over her chest defensively.

"First of all, I wanted to say I'm sorry. I had absolutely no idea you worked here." Brock's sincere expression didn't succeed in soothing her annoyance. Maybe she had noticed the shock in his eyes when he'd recognized her, but she was the one who'd lost a sister. "I moved home for family reasons, not to torment you."

"Doesn't matter to me where you work," she said in a stiff, formal tone. "You stay out of my way, and I'll stay out of yours."

He stared at her for a long moment, and she struggled not to squirm beneath his intense scrutiny. She could see why Raine had called him steamy hot. He wore his chocolate-brown hair a little longer than was fashionable, but with his chiseled jaw and strong chin he was ruggedly attractive. To everyone else, maybe. Not to her. "If that's what you want. But it might help if we could spend some time talking things through."

Talk things through? She blinked. Was he serious? The nerve of him acting as though talking things out would somehow bring Felicity back. She curled her fingers into fists, her nails digging into the palm of her hand, and for a moment she relished the tiny flash of pain.

Maybe they had to work together, but, as far as she was concerned, there would never be anything remotely personal between them.

"No. I don't think so."

He frowned. "Why not?"

"Because there is absolutely nothing you have to say that I want to hear." With that, she turned, leaving a gaping Brock standing behind her as she walked away.

CHAPTER TWO

FINISHING her shift, while being stuck in the trauma bay with Brock Madison, was the hardest thing Elana had had to do since moving into her first foster home at the tender age of fifteen.

He'd wanted to talk things through.

Yeah. Right. To make himself feel better, no doubt.

Elana swallowed hard, trying without success to keep from ruminating over Brock Madison. Even when he wasn't in the immediate area, she'd found herself searching for him. If only so she could find a way to stay as far away from him as possible.

Raine was right: Brock was devastatingly attractive. Too much so. In those brief moments when he'd pinned her with his sizzling blue gaze, she'd nearly forgotten how much she hated him.

Brock had matured over the years. She shouldn't have been surprised; it wasn't as if she was the same angry and confused fifteen-year-old, either. But for some reason, her brain had always pictured him as the young, reckless college student who'd been speeding down the highway when Felicity pulled out in front of him.

For years she'd railed against the unfairness of it all. Brock had essentially walked away from the crash with only a couple of minor injuries—a broken collarbone and a few cracked ribs—while Felicity had died at the scene.

Enough. She needed to stop wallowing in the past. She threw herself into her work with a vengeance. Elana thought she'd successfully hidden her feelings towards Brock, but at the end of their shift, Raine cornered her in the staff lounge.

"All right, give. What is up with you and Dr Madison?"

Elana raised a brow, trying to keep her expression impassive. "Nothing."

Raine rolled her eyes. "Yeah, sure, and I'm Princess Stephanie. Come on, Elana. It's obvious you two know each other. For one thing, he called you by name before anyone had introduced you. And then he followed you to the staff lounge to talk to you in private. Did the two of you have a relationship in the past or what?"

Relationship? Good Lord, nothing could be further from the truth. "No. I barely know the guy."

"I don't believe you." Raine swiped her badge through the time clock, and Elana followed suit. "I'm not blind. There's a definite tension between you."

Elana suppressed a sigh, knowing Raine would continue to badger her endlessly unless she explained. "Remember when I told you my sister died in a car crash nine years ago?"

Raine frowned. "Yes." Then her eyes rounded. "Was your sister dating Brock at the time?"

"No. Worse." Elana walked into the staff locker room to retrieve her purse. She slammed the locker door shut with more force than was necessary. "Brock was the driver of the car that hit her."

"No! Really?" Raine's mouth dropped open in disbelief. "You have got to be kidding me."

"I wish I was." Elana's expression was grim, and she dropped onto the bench, her shoulders slumping with sudden fatigue. Keeping up the pretense that everything was okay when it really wasn't had been exhausting. "I don't know if I can do this, Raine," she whispered. "I don't think I can work with him."

Raine sat down beside her, putting a comforting arm around her shoulders. "Don't make any rash decisions, Elana. I'm sure this has been a shock, but Brock Madison seems to be a really good doctor. Maybe you need to give him a chance."

Give him a chance? Why? What about Felicity's chance? Her sister's life had ended far too young, and it was all Brock's fault.

She didn't want to give him a chance. Logically, Elana knew Raine might be right, since Chloe would have told her the same thing. But letting go of the past wasn't easy. Those dark years after her sister's death had been so awful. She winced and rubbed her pounding temple. "I can't," she murmured.

"Elana, you can. You're an adult now, and you're

strong. Remember I'm always here for you if you need to talk." Raine gave her a quick hug. "Call me anytime."

Elana flashed a weak smile. "Thanks."

They gathered their things and headed outside to the staff parking lot. The night air was chilly for April, and she hunched her shoulders against the breeze, having left her coat in the car in her rush to get to work on time.

That night Elana couldn't sleep. Because there was no way she was going to be able to work with Brock. And she mourned the fact that her career as a trauma nurse was likely over.

"Brock? Do you have a minute?"

Elana's voice made him stop and turn in amazement. She'd called out to him. Voluntarily. Her dark eyes were warm and welcoming, making her even more beautiful than the first time he'd seen her at work. "Elana. It's great to see you."

Her tremulous smile made his chest tighten with anticipation. "I've been looking all over for you, Brock. I wanted to say I'm sorry. I'm so sorry for the way I treated you the other day. I had no right to be angry with you."

"I—don't know what to say. Does this mean you've forgiven me?" He could barely allow himself to hope.

She smiled. "Yes, Brock. I forgive you."

The incessant ringing of his phone pulled him from the dream. With a low groan of regret, Brock pried his eyes open, searching for his cell phone. Whoever was calling him this early in the morning had better have a good reason.

He'd wanted to stay asleep. To spend more time with the Elana in his dreams. The beautiful, smiling Elana who didn't blame him for her sister's death.

"Yeah?" He opened his phone without looking at the screen to see who was calling.

"Brock? You gotta help me, man." He could barely hear his younger brother Joel's voice over the shrill wailing of a baby in the background. "I can't take it any more. Tucker's crying non-stop. There has to be something wrong with him. Something bad. He cries all the time!"

Wincing at the desperation in his brother's tone, he swung out of bed. Joel had got his girlfriend, Lacey, pregnant, and while Brock admired his brother's efforts, Joel was obviously struggling in his attempt to do the right thing. "Try to relax. Babies can sense when something is wrong. Tucker is only seven weeks old; maybe he's a little colicky. Does he seem better riding in the car? Or in the baby swing?"

"No. Nothing works." Joel's tone rose in agitation. "He just cries and cries. I'm telling you, there's something seriously wrong!"

Brock scrubbed a hand over his chin. Joel was only twenty-two, but his girlfriend, Lacey, was even younger, just six months past nineteen. They were young and finding it difficult to handle the responsibility of a brand-new family. Hence Brock's decision to move back to Milwaukee. Especially after hearing their father had refused to offer Joel any financial help. He felt bad for Joel. The screaming baby in the background was already getting on his nerves, and he wasn't there with them. "All right, maybe there is something going on with the baby other than just colic. You and Lacey need to take Tucker to the doctor for a check-up."

"We thought you could look at him," Joel said. "Since neither of us has health insurance."

"There's a low-income family clinic that caters for mothers and babies in Lacey's position," Brock explained patiently. "I don't mind taking a look at Tucker, but I'm not a peds expert. And I can't run lab tests on him to see if he has some sort of infection. Or do a chest X-ray of his lungs if he needs one. You could bring him to the ED while I'm working, but that will end up costing you more than simply going to the clinic. I really think you should go where they can offer the most help."

"All right. Where is this so-called clinic?" Joel asked in defeat.

Brock gave him the directions, wondering if the hospital had failed to give Lacey this information after she'd given birth. They certainly should have done more to help these two young kids, especially knowing Lacey's financial situation. They'd qualify for food support as well as basic health-care needs.

"You're going to be fine, Joel," he tried to reassure his brother.

"I don't know," Joel protested. "I'm not as strong as you, Brock."

"Yes, you are." He wished he could give his brother the self-confidence he needed. "You're stronger than you know."

"I'll talk to you later," Joel said evasively.

He didn't push, knowing Joel was under a huge amount of stress. Their father had basically tossed Joel onto the street. Brock had helped them move into a small duplex apartment and paid the security deposit along with the first three months of rent. Joel was only working part-time at a gas station, so Brock had also been trying to help his brother find a full-time job, one that would ideally provide decent benefits. Raising a child in this day and age without health insurance was not easy.

He stared at his phone. Should he have offered to take Tucker to the clinic? No, as much as he wanted to help his brother, he couldn't do everything for Joel. His brother would become more self-confident if he grew up a bit and took some responsibility.

After tossing his cell phone back down on his discarded clothes, Brock flopped back down on his bed, throwing his arm up over his eyes. He wished he could fall back asleep, picking up the dream with Elana where he'd left off. For a few brief moments, her forgiveness had swept away the dark cloud of guilt, making him feel light-hearted and happy.

But it was only a dream. In reality, Elana hadn't forgiven him for the accident that had stolen her sister's life. And, considering the way their conversation had ended so abruptly yesterday, he had to acknowledge she never would.

He knew he needed to let it go, but the sting of her rejection continued to gnaw at him. Why he was letting it bother him, he had no idea. He'd carried the guilt of that night for a long time. Had changed his major to medicine the semester after the accident, vowing to make a difference in other people's lives.

He'd also done what he could for Elana. More than she realized. Yet nothing he could do would bring Felicity back.

Her sister's death had haunted him for years. No reason for that to change now.

The best thing he could do for Elana was to stay far away from her. He'd caused her enough pain. He refused to cause any more.

Elana hadn't slept well, but her fatigue didn't keep her in bed for long. Today was Wednesday, the day she was scheduled to work a four-hour stint volunteering at the low-income family clinic providing care to people who didn't have access to better health care.

Normally she enjoyed her hours at the clinic, as there was something immensely satisfying about helping people in need. Some of the cases were heart-wrenching, the pregnant mothers trying to overcome their addictions, or the young people who'd contracted HIV, but there were also a lot of people who just needed a helping hand.

Today her head pounded with a dull ache she'd had ever since she'd woken up that morning. No doubt a result of a restless night, which was all Brock Madison's fault.

But she wasn't going to think about him. Brock was just another ED doctor she'd have to work with. And if he liked trauma, then maybe she'd ask Stacey to assign her to one of the arena teams for a while. At least until she figured out what her options were.

Staying in the ED long-term was clearly not going to work. She needed to find a new career and fast.

Shaking off her depressing thoughts, Elana drove her tiny compact car down to the clinic. The clinic was in the middle of the low-income district, several miles from her tiny apartment. The clinic had to be close to where people in need lived because many of these clients didn't have cars or other means of reliable transportation.

Finding a parking space was always a challenge. As she walked inside the clinic, she discovered Tina Kaplan was the receptionist on duty.

"Hi, Tina. How are you today?"

"Great, Elana. How is your aunt Chloe doing?"

All of the staff at the New Beginnings Clinic knew Chloe, her foster mother, had volunteered her time here as a receptionist while Elana was growing up. Elana was glad that she could now return the favor, carrying on her foster mother's tradition. "She's wonderful. The cardiac stent went very well."

"I'm so glad." Tina handed over the list of patients who were already waiting to be seen. Their clients often began lining up at the door a half hour before the clinic officially opened.

"Me too." Elana took the list and scanned it, as always checking to see which of her previous clients might be making a return visit. "Thanks, Tina. Who's the doctor coming in today?"

"Hmm." Tina glanced up at the handwritten schedule. "Looks like Liz Jacoby is the MD on the schedule today."

Liz was an exceptionally talented African-American woman who donated a lot of her time to the New Beginnings Clinic. Most of their clients didn't know that Liz Jacoby was also a nationally renowned breast cancer physician. Elana loved working with her. Her dull headache began to fade. "Excellent. We should have a good day, then."

"When do you want me to start sending patients back?" Tina asked.

"Give me five minutes to make sure everything is well stocked, and then you can let 'em rip."

Tina laughed, and Elana smiled as she headed back to the exam room. She routinely saw the patients first and then got the physician involved in their care as needed. Their system would have worked better with more volunteers, but so far, other than Raine, she hadn't convinced any of her other co-workers to help by donating their time.

The first few patients came through with simple enough concerns. One woman had a bad cough with a fever that Elana suspected was a case of bronchitis turning into pneumonia. The next two patients were severely dehydrated from the stomach flu that was making its way through the city. Another young man came in with a serious burn on his forearm, with a story she absolutely did not believe.

"Jackson, there is no way you got this burn from a lighter falling on your arm," she told him sternly. "Do you really think I'm that stupid? I can tell this is a gasoline burn. So why don't you tell me what really happened?"

The young man refused to talk. Elana sighed and applied a generous amount of ointment to the burn, wrapping it with gauze to keep it clean and dry. Maybe Liz would be able to pry more information out of the taciturn young man.

"Elana?" Tina called from the other side of the door.

"Yes?"

"How much longer? There's a young woman and a crying baby that need to get in to see you right away."

That didn't sound too good. She reached over and opened the door. "I'm nearly finished. Jackson just needs to see Dr Jacoby while I get his wound supplies together."

"I'll do it. Tell me what he needs."

Elana raised a brow. "What's going on? Is the baby that sick?"

"I don't know, but the mother is crying almost as hard as the baby." Tina's eyes were full of compassionate concern. "I can't stand it."

"All right, get him ten rolls of gauze and a jar of burns cream. Jackson, you need to change this dressing twice a day and return here to the clinic in five days, do you understand? We need to make sure that burn doesn't get infected."

"Yes, ma'am."

Tina hustled the young man out of the exam room, taking him over to see the doctor. Elana quickly threw out the paper strip from the exam table and wiped down the surface with a disposable bleach cloth. Within two minutes, a young waif-thin girl lugging a crying baby on her shoulder came into the room.

"Good morning, I'm the nurse here, my name is Elana. What's going on today?"

The young woman's eyes were swollen and red from her weeping. "He just keeps crying and crying. I don't know what I'm doing wrong," she murmured.

"There now, I'm sure it's nothing you're doing wrong," Elana said firmly. "What's your name? Do you mind if I hold him for a minute?"

Letting out a loud sniffle, the young woman handed the baby over. "I'm Lacey, and his name is Tucker. He's seven weeks old."

"Hi, Tucker," Elana crooned, gently nuzzling the baby, testing the temperature of his skin. He did feel warm, but that could just as easily be because of the crying. She loved babies, another reason she volunteered her time here. Giving him one last nuzzle, she laid him on the exam table and undid his diaper, looking for obvious signs of irritation, like diaper rash, before using her stethoscope to listen to his heart and lungs.

Not an easy task while he was crying.

"Are you breast-feeding?" Elana asked, her heart going out to the waif-thin girl. The baby sounded a bit congested, but it could be merely the result of his non-stop crying. His ears didn't look red, ruling out an ear infection.

"No. We give him whatever formula is on sale at the store," Lacey admitted.

"That might be your problem," Elana said gently. "Colicky babies don't tolerate dairy-based formula, and you should really stick to one brand. I want you to try the soy-based formula, and nothing else. I'll give you some free samples here."

"Are you sure it's nothing more serious?" Lacey asked, swiping her nose on her sleeve. The motion pushed up the sleeve of her shirt, revealing a few bloody cuts on her forearm. As if she sensed Elana's gaze, she quickly covered the area back up again. "I can't believe Tucker is crying this much just because of colic."

Elana wanted to ask about the suspicious marks she saw on Lacey's arm, but at the moment little Tucker was her primary concern. "Don't underestimate colic, Lacey. I've seen many mothers reduced to tears over inconsolably crying babies. There are many ways to treat colic. First let me get a soy-based formula sample for you to try, okay?"

Lacey sniffled again and nodded.

"I'll be right back." Elana handed her the baby and hurried over to their jam-packed supply cabinet and found a six-pack of soy-based cans of formula and a disposable bottle. After quickly preparing the bottle, she brought it back to the exam room.

"Here, see if he'll take this," she instructed.

Lacey held the baby in the crook of her arm and tried the bottle. At first Tucker sucked greedily, then, after a few minutes, he turned his head away and began crying again.

"See how he's hungry but then turns away? That's another classic sign of colic, too much gas. We can give him some anti-gas medicine in an eyedropper that should work. And I will get Dr Jacoby to take a listen to him just to be sure there's nothing else going on."

Elana hesitated and then carefully asked, "Do you have anyone to help you, Lacey? Or are you raising Tucker all alone?"

Lacey shrugged, trying to get Tucker to take the bottle again. "Joel, the baby's father, is trying to help me, but he can't stand it when Tucker cries."

Oh, boy. Sounded like Joel and Lacey needed a lot of help. And she couldn't dismiss those cuts on Lacey's arms. She understood how hopelessness could suffocate your soul.

"Lacey, I'm here for you. I'd like you to come back in two days and bring Joel with you. You both need to learn how to deal with a colicky baby. I've heard using a baby swing alongside a noisy vacuum cleaner works, and car rides. Once Tucker gets the dairy products out of his system and starts on the anti-gas medication, he should be better."

"Joel's brother is a doctor, and even he thought there might be something more wrong with the baby," Lacey said defensively.

She frowned at Lacey's tone. Did the poor girl feel as if she wasn't a good mother because she couldn't handle the baby's crying? "Really? Is his brother a pediatric specialist?"

"No, but Brock works in the emergency department at Trinity Medical Center."

Brock? Had she heard correctly? Her stomach clenched, and she forced herself to ask, "What's Joel's last name?"

"Madison. Joel Madison."

CHAPTER THREE

Later that day, Elana couldn't stop thinking about Lacey's plight. The cuts on that poor girl's forearm haunted her. Lacey needed help. For herself and for her baby. More than just a quick clinic visit.

No matter how much she wanted to stay far away from Brock, she simply couldn't ignore her conscience. Lacey was obviously in serious trouble; the telltale cuts on her forearm were not to be taken lightly. And Tucker was Brock's nephew. Hadn't Brock mentioned that he'd moved home to deal with some family issues?

There was no way around it. She needed to talk to Brock. To let him know her concerns about Lacey, Joel and their baby.

When she arrived at work, she walked into the arena and was surprised to discover they were busier than usual for a Wednesday evening. Patients streamed in seemingly from nowhere.

She couldn't deny a hint of relief at the reprieve. There was no time to talk to anyone, not when so many patients were in need of assistance. She jumped into the fray, helping to move patients through the system. But just when they'd started to catch up, a local discount store reported a serious gas leak. Dozens of people flooded the ED to be ruled out for potential carbon monoxide poisoning.

Luckily, most of the discount store patrons weren't too sick, but each patient had to be registered, screened, treated and released, taking up a significant amount of time and energy. Elana had been pulled from the trauma bay to help, giving her what should have been a welcome break from working with Brock Madison.

Except she still really needed to talk to him about Lacey. At least, that was what she told herself when she found she was constantly looking for him.

"Do we have any more carbon monoxide poisoning cases left?" Raine asked, coming over to stand beside Elana, who was finishing up the charting on her soon-to-be-discharged patient. "Because if I don't get a chance to eat something soon, I'm going to pass out myself."

"I don't think so," Elana said, glancing up at the central board listing the status of all their patients. "According to Stacey, we were expecting to see twenty-three patients, and I'm sure we've moved at least that many through already."

"I hope so," Raine muttered with a low groan. "At least this influx of patients has made the shift go by fast."

"No kidding. Why don't you take a break? I'll cover for you," Elana offered. "Then, when you're finished, I'll go."

"Thanks. Give me at least fifteen minutes."

"Take twenty," Elana said generously. "We deserve it."

Even though the immediate urgency of the discount store gas leak had passed, there were still quite a few patients to see. Since the trauma bay was quiet, Elana continued to help out in the arena.

When she nearly tripped over Brock, she realized Stacey had reassigned Brock to the arena too. Probably to help with the influx of patients.

"Elana? Can you send a pregnancy test on the female patient in room two?" he asked.

"Sure. Is she one of the carbon monoxide exposure patients?"

He nodded. "She's a bit worried she might be pregnant."

Understandable. She hurried over to do what he'd asked. Unfortunately there wasn't time to ask him about Lacey because her second patient began complaining of tight chest pain.

"I think you'd better take a look at this guy, Mr Reeves, in room eighteen," she told Brock. "He has new-onset chest pain; we just did an ECG and sent labs. I think he needs to be moved into the trauma bay."

Brock didn't hesitate. "Let's take a look."

The elderly gentleman had come in originally because of a fall, but now, with this new onset of chest pain, Elana guessed it was more likely his fall had been caused by his heart problems in the first place.

"Definitely signs of ST depression, according to his twelve-lead ECG," Brock murmured. "Let's get him into the trauma bay so we have more access to equipment. I'll call Cardiology so we can get this guy into the cath lab asap."

Elana nodded, quickly explaining to Mr Reeves their plan. When she asked about his support systems, she learned his wife had passed away a year ago from colon cancer and he had two kids, a son and a daughter. He didn't want to bother his kids, though, claiming they had their own families to worry about.

"I really think we need to call them," she urged. "You may be having a small heart attack. I'm sure your son and daughter would want to know." And hopefully they were decent kids who would come in to support their father.

Mr Reeves grudgingly agreed, and Elana quickly called the son, Kirk, who willingly took responsibility for getting in touch with his sister, Lisa. Satisfied her elderly patient wouldn't be alone for long, she hurried back to his side.

"Your son, Kirk, is on his way," she told him. "And he's going to call Lisa too."

"Thanks," he whispered. His face had gone pale, and there was a fine sheen of sweat on his brow.

"Are you having more pain?" she asked in concern.

"Maybe a little," he grudgingly admitted.

Catching Brock's eye, she waved him over. "Mr Reeves is having pain; can I give him more morphine?"

"Absolutely. Give him five milligrams and move up to ten as needed. Draw a troponin level if you haven't already. The cardiologist is on his way down."

"I already drew the troponin with the rest of the labs; we should have the results any minute." She hurried over to the medication machine to withdraw the narcotics for her patient.

Mr Reeves visibly relaxed after he received the additional pain medication. His troponin level was elevated, so the cardiologist wasted no time in arranging for transport to the cardiac cath lab.

"Wait," Mr Reeves protested. "I need to wait for my son."

"You can't wait, Mr Reeves," Elana said gently. "There isn't time; the quicker they can get your heart fixed, the less damage you'll have. I promise I'll talk to Kirk when he gets here. Your son will be in the waiting room when you're all finished, okay?"

"Okay," he reluctantly agreed.

"Nice job," Brock murmured as the cardiology team wheeled Mr Reeves away. "You handled that very well."

His offhand praise made her blush. "Er, thanks." They'd been so busy since the start of their shift, the stilted awkwardness between them from the day before had vanished. She wasn't sure it was a good thing. Could she really just pretend Felicity's death meant nothing?

No. But at the same time, there were other, more important things to worry about. Like the situation with Lacey, Tucker and Brock's brother.

Gathering her courage, she looked him in the eye. "Brock, do you have a few minutes after our shift to talk?"

He looked surprised, but readily agreed. "Of course. I can be available at any time you need."

His eagerness made her feel guilty. Did he think they were going to rehash the past? Not likely. She hesitated, wondering if maybe she should give him a hint as to what she wanted to discuss.

"Elana, I'm glad you're willing to talk to me," Brock said in a low voice before she could think of a way to ease into the topic of his brother. "I haven't been able to get you out of my mind."

Really? Her cheeks felt hot all over again, and she cursed herself for succumbing to his charm. She wasn't the least bit attracted to Brock Madison, and she didn't need his approval to feel confident in her nursing skills.

"Elana? I'm back," Raine said, walking up to them. "It's your turn to take a break."

She took the chance to escape gratefully. "Thanks, I'm starved. See you later," she said to Brock before hurrying away.

Good grief, she needed to pull herself together, and quick. The purpose of her chat with Brock was solely to explain her concerns about Lacey and Tucker.

Once she'd let Brock know what was going on with Lacey and Tucker, she'd have no reason to speak to him on a personal level again.

Brock couldn't control the wide grin on his face as he either helped dispatch patients home or admitted them to the hospital, depending on the extent of their illness.

Even though he doubted that Elana was totally going to let him off the hook the way she had in his dreams, he was thrilled she was finally going to give him a chance to explain.

Nine years ago he'd gone to Felicity's funeral, but

that attempt to talk to Elana and her mother had ended in disaster. Her mother had all but tossed him out of the church, creating such a scene that he'd escaped before the police were called.

Good thing, since his policeman father had nearly boxed his ears after the accident as it was.

Months later, he'd tried to talk to them again, only to find Elana's mother's house was for sale. He'd soon discovered Louisa had suffered a complete nervous breakdown and Elana had been placed in foster care.

Shaken by the events that seemed to keep getting worse instead of better, he'd made it his business from that point forward to keep tabs on Elana from afar. Guilt had been his constant companion during those months following the accident, despite the results of Felicity's autopsy. Those seconds before she'd pulled out in front of him had replayed over and over in his mind.

When he'd entered medical school, he'd buried his guilt and poured his energies into his studies. He'd graduated top of his class, but he couldn't have cared less.

He'd been determined to save lives. It was the only way he could live with himself.

Brock took a ten-minute break, checking his phone for voice mail messages, surprised to find a message from Lacey. She'd sounded upset, crying again, as she'd begged him to call her back.

Glancing at his watch, he realized she'd called almost thirty minutes ago. Wincing at the delay, he quickly dialed her number, hoping she hadn't gotten bad news regarding Tucker's health.

"Lacey? It's Brock. What's wrong?"

"Oh, Brock, I don't know what to do. Joel's gone," Lacey said between hiccupping sobs.

Brock frowned. "What do you mean, he's gone? Gone to work? Is there something wrong with Tucker?"

"I took Tucker to the clinic, like you said. They did some tests, gave me medicine for him and told me to use different formula because he probably has colic. When I came home, I thought Joel was at work, but a couple of hours ago, they called here looking for him."

A warning chill snaked down his back. Joel couldn't have taken off, could he? Surely he wouldn't risk losing his job, not when he had a baby to support. "Okay, don't panic," he said soothingly, hiding the depth of his concern. "I know Joel has been having a tough time lately. He probably just needed a little break. He's likely having a drink or two with a couple of his buddies."

"That's what I thought too, at first," Lacey said. "But I've called all his friends—no one has seen him all day. I even went to the bowling alley, his favorite hangout, but he hasn't been there either. I'm scared, Brock. What am I going to do if he's gone for good?"

Elana swiped out at the end of her shift and then glanced around, searching for Brock. He'd promised to meet her in the staff lounge after work, but it was possible he was still finishing up. The physicians couldn't leave until they were assured all the patients were safe. The hand-over of care was easier for the nurses, though, since there were more nurses assigned per shift than doctors.

Nervous, she swiped her damp palms on the sides of her scrubs. A brief conversation with Brock shouldn't cause an anxiety attack. Especially since this talk wasn't remotely personal. This was about Lacey. The young mother and her son hadn't been far from her thoughts all evening.

"Do you want to walk out to the parking lot together?" Raine asked.

"Nah, go ahead without me. I have a few things I have to do yet," Elana hedged, avoiding direct eye contact with her closest friend.

"Like what?" Raine demanded, oblivious to Elana's subtle hint. "You've swiped out, haven't you? What else is there to do? It's not like you can make phone calls or run errands at eleven-thirty at night."

Elana suppressed a sigh. "There was a patient at the clinic today that has me worried. I need a few minutes to run the issue past Brock, that's all."

"Oh. I see." Elana didn't appreciate the knowing glint in Raine's eye. "I'm sure *Brock* will be more than happy to help you out."

"It's not like that, Raine," she snapped. "This isn't a personal issue. I barely know the man."

Raine arched one brow in disbelief. "Sure, Elana. Whatever you say. Heck, I think it's great you're talking to him. That means you're giving him a chance. Hey, maybe you can get him to volunteer a few shifts a month at the clinic too."

Oh, no. Absolutely not. No way was she asking Brock to volunteer at the clinic. Working with him in the emergency department was bad enough. The clinic was her refuge. She didn't want him anywhere near the place.

After Raine had finally left, she let out a sigh of relief and plopped into a chair to wait for Brock. She'd give him another five minutes before she went searching for him. She was tired and didn't have all night.

Yet she refused to leave without telling him her concerns about Lacey.

When he finally came in, he looked terrible. He wasn't smiling, his face drawn into harsh lines. He looked about as exhausted as she felt.

For a minute she wavered. Maybe this wasn't exactly the time to dump her concerns on him.

But just as quickly she stiffened her resolve. This wasn't about Brock; he could take care of himself. Tucker was the vulnerable one. Not that Lacey was an awful mother, but she was definitely struggling.

"Hi, Elana. Sorry I'm late," Brock said with a forced smile.

"No problem. It was a rough night for everyone, I think." Making small talk with Brock felt weird. Truthfully, until the day they'd worked together in the trauma room, they hadn't exchanged more than half a dozen words to each other, and none of them pleasant or friendly. At least on her part.

A hint of embarrassment crept under her skin when she remembered how she'd lashed out at him all those years ago at Felicity's funeral. She pushed the memories of the past aside.

She cleared her throat, swiping her hands on her

scrubs again. "I'm sorry to bother you, but there's a problem I think you need to know about."

His dark brows pulled together in a frown. "A problem?"

"Yes. I volunteer at the New Beginnings Clinic down in the low-income district. Earlier today, a very distraught young woman brought in her colicky baby to be evaluated by the doctor."

Brock's spine straightened, and the expression on his face became noncommittal. "Lacey and Tucker."

She was surprised he'd guessed, but that only made it easier to speak her mind. "Yes. You need to know I'm really concerned about them. Especially Lacey."

"Why? Because there was something wrong with Tucker? She's not hurting him or anything is she?" Brock asked in a rush.

"No! No, it's not that." Although she could understand why he might jump to that conclusion. Working in the ED, they sometimes saw cases of child abuse. "Tucker has a bad case of colic, but she was making it worse by giving him different kinds of formula. I helped her switch him over to a soy-based product and gave her some anti-gas medication for him. But your brother, the baby's father, didn't come to the appointment with her."

Brock's shoulders slumped with apparent relief that abuse wasn't the issue. "Yeah, I'm not surprised," he muttered.

He was being far to blasé about the entire situation. She leaned forward, willing him to understand. "Listen to me. I noticed several small cuts on Lacey's arm. She covered them up right away, but I didn't imagine them. She's not coping very well with motherhood. I think she might be cutting herself, purposefully inflicting pain."

"What?" Brock stared at her in disbelief. "Are you telling me she's suicidal?"

Elana didn't want to have this conversation, she really didn't. But hadn't she learned the hard way how ignoring a problem only made it worse? "Young adults who are known to be cutters aren't suicidal per se, but it is a sign of being unable to cope. They cut themselves because it's one area of their life they can actually control. And cutting themselves seems to help relieve guilt, in a bizarre way."

"You sound like you're familiar with this affliction," Brock said, his gaze intense.

She swallowed hard. She knew far more than she wanted to about kids who used harmful ways to cope. Been there and done that.

And it was all Brock's fault.

For a moment darkness threatened. She pushed the sensation away. "I know a little about it."

"I see." He stared at her, a flash of real regret intermixed with guilt shadowing his eyes. Could it be that the accident had affected him more than she realized?

Disturbed by the possibility, she stared down at her hands. Had Brock really suffered too? Maybe, but so what? He'd been able to walk away. She hadn't. Besides, she needed to focus on the issue at hand.

Lacey and Tucker.

"Brock, you need to make your brother understand

how his son needs him. Joel and Lacey should take a parenting class; there are resources to help them." She silently pleaded with him to take her advice seriously. "I honestly don't think Lacey is stable enough, or capable enough to raise Tucker alone."

"Yeah, well, unfortunately, that's going to be a problem," Brock admitted, his expression grim. "Lacey just called me less than an hour ago. She's freaking out because apparently my brother, Joel, went AWOL. She hasn't seen him all day, and no one seems to know where he is."

CHAPTER FOUR

"LACEY has been home alone with Tucker all day?" Elana couldn't control the surge of panic as she stared at Brock in horror. "We have to get over there right away."

"Maybe you're right." He glanced at her, his gaze serious. "I know it's a lot to ask, but since you've established a bond with Lacey, she might feel better if you came along."

She hesitated and then steeled her resolve. Lacey needed her. "Of course I'll come with you."

"Thanks."

Ten minutes later she found herself seated in the passenger seat of Brock's SUV as he drove to Lacey's small duplex. She twisted her hands in her lap and stole a glimpse at him. His gaze was glued to the road, his face drawn into a deep frown. She found it difficult to breathe; his presence was large and overpowering in the tight confines of the car.

There was no way to know what was going through his mind. She told herself she didn't care, but couldn't quite make herself believe it. He'd immediately jumped to help Lacey, and she was reluctantly impressed with his willingness to do whatever was necessary.

The silence was deafening. For the life of her, she couldn't think of anything to say. She barely knew him. Brock the emergency medicine physician was a complete enigma to her.

Not that she'd known Brock the reckless college student either.

Her aunt Chloe had discouraged her from blindly believing the rumors about Brock's speeding. The normal speed limit on that stretch of highway where the accident had occurred was forty-five miles per hour. More than fast enough to have caused a fatal accident without speeding.

Elana had refused to listen. It was easier to hate Brock for her messed-up life than to hate her disabled mother. Or her dead sister.

She glanced at the dashboard, noticing he drove well within the speed limit. Of course, she would too if she'd caused a young girl to die.

Her chest tightened with a spurt of empathy. How awful to know you'd taken a life. She couldn't imagine how difficult that must have been.

Wait a minute. Why was she feeling sorry for Brock? His guilt, one way or the other, wasn't her concern.

Turning her attention to Lacey and Tucker, she glanced at the clock. Almost midnight. Did Brock know where to find his brother, Joel? She hoped so. She wouldn't mind staying with Lacey while he went searching for him.

Brock pulled into the driveway of a rather dilapidated building a few minutes later. The lights were on in the upper-level apartment, and Brock softly rapped on the door, as if trying not to wake the occupants of the lower apartment.

Lacey answered the door a few minutes later. There was no sign of Tucker, which caused a tingle of alarm to skate down Elana's back.

For Brock too, apparently, because the first thing he said was, "Where's the baby?"

"Sleeping." Lacey seemed surprised yet happy to see Elana. "Come in."

They trooped up the stairs to the apartment. The interior was a bit of a mess, clothes scattered around and dirty dishes piled on top of the scarred coffee table. Elana's fingers itched to clean up. Instead she turned her back on the mess, facing Tucker's young mother.

"Hi, Lacey. Do you remember me from the clinic? My name is Elana, and I work with Brock in the emergency department."

Lacey slowly nodded. "I remember. The gas medicine seems to be helping. Tucker napped for a full two hours this afternoon."

Elana smiled. "I'm so glad. I'm sure the new formula will help too."

"Do you mind if we look in on the baby?" Brock asked, still wearing his scowling frown. "We promise not to wake him."

Lacey lifted a thin shoulder in a half shrug. "I guess. He's probably going to wake up in another hour or so anyway to eat. He's been getting up to eat every four hours."

The resigned expression on the young woman's face bothered Elana. Was Lacey already imaging what it was going to be like to raise Tucker all by herself? She was glad the woman didn't seem too desperate, yet she also knew how easy it was to hide your true feelings.

She darted a glance at Brock, and he nodded at her unspoken question, gesturing towards the bedroom door that Lacey had left partially open. She tiptoed into Tucker's room, gazing down at the sleeping baby nestled in the crib, lying on his back, with a rolled-up blanket tucked behind him.

Brock and Lacey spoke in low tones, no doubt discussing where Joel might be. She longed to pick up the baby, but knew better than to disturb the sleeping infant. If Lacey was right, he'd be awake soon enough anyway.

She left the room quietly, closing the door soundlessly behind her. "He seems to be sleeping pretty well," she announced, coming back into the living room.

Brock was on his cell phone, calling one of Joel's friends. After several fruitless calls, he snapped his phone shut in defeat.

"I'm sorry, Lacey. There's nothing more I can do to find him tonight," he said in a resigned tone.

Lacey looked as if she wanted to cry. "I know."

Brock let out a heavy sigh. "Go and pack a bag full of whatever you and the baby will need for a few days," he said. "You and Tucker will be better off staying at my place until we find my brother."

* * *

Brock sat on Lacey's sofa, broodingly watching as Lacey began packing their things together. He didn't mind helping out, but he couldn't quell a sense of panic. Moving Lacey and Tucker to his place was a drastic step. What if they didn't find Joel right away? How long would this arrangement have to last? He didn't have any idea, but he also didn't have any other options. He couldn't leave Lacey to cope on her own.

Dammit, where in the hell was Joel?

Brock had to swallow his seething frustration. He couldn't help being annoyed with his brother. He'd come home to give Joel a helping hand, but Joel needed to do his part too. Disappearing was not holding up his end of the deal.

He scrubbed a hand over his jaw. Had their dad been right to deny Joel any financial help after the baby was born? Maybe Brock's offer to help was only enabling Joel to shirk his responsibilities.

No. Joel needed support. And Elana's concerns were well founded. It was no secret to him that Lacey was having trouble coping, but he hadn't realized the full extent of her problems. Deliberately cutting herself in some twisted need to be in control was scary.

And how had Elana known those sorts of details? Just from working as a nurse in the emergency department or because of her own troubled teenage years?

It was difficult to think about how Elana had struggled back then, losing her sister and then her mother. She'd certainly been a casualty in the entire mess. He'd hoped that Elana was ready to talk, had foolishly looked forward to their meeting after work, only to be taken aback by her concerns regarding Lacey and Tucker.

How long had she been working at the New Beginnings Clinic? He couldn't help admiring her willingness to help those in need. Patients like Lacey would certainly flourish under her care. Elana was a beautiful woman, inside and out. He was amazed at how accomplished she was. Selfishly, he wished he could get to know Elana better.

But that wasn't likely.

Tucker woke up, crying softly at first but then swinging into a full-blown wail. Lacey became flustered, dropping her bag and rushing over to him as if something awful would happen if the baby cried too long.

"Here, why don't you let me take care of him for you," Elana said, following Lacey into the bedroom. "That way you can keep gathering all your stuff together."

Brock wondered if he should offer to help too, but when Elana changed the baby's diapers and competently whisked him off to the kitchen to make a bottle, he decided she had things under control.

The way Elana cooed at his nephew, pressing kisses to the top of his head even as he cried, captured his gaze. When she finally settled down in the rocking chair, quieting the baby with the bottle, a bolt of desire shot straight to his groin.

What in the world was wrong with him? He'd no business thinking of Elana in a personal way, as a woman he might be interested in. Yet, suddenly, he couldn't tear his eyes from the picture she made gazing serenely at Tucker. Since when did he get aroused watching a beautiful woman rock a baby?

Since never. He must be overly tired. Talk about being self-destructive. Elana hated him. Being attracted to her was crazy. She deserved a family of her own.

But he didn't. There was no way he'd ever consider having children. Ever.

He tore his gaze away and jumped to his feet. He needed to do something. Anything. When he saw Lacey lugging the swing towards the door, he bit back a protest and crossed over to take it from her.

"I'll carry that down to the car for you," he said quickly. "Does it fold up somehow?"

"I think so. Joel put it together for me," Lacey said.

Wrestling with the baby swing gave him something to do. But, even so, he found his gaze resting on Elana and Tucker more than once.

When he saw the amount of stuff Lacey was packing, including the swing, a portable cradle, the infant car seat, the box of diapers and their suitcases full of clothes, a surge of panic grabbed him by the throat. He'd only asked her to come for a few days, not to move in permanently.

He was going to kill Joel when he found him. No, scratch that plan; he couldn't kill his brother because then Lacey and Tucker would really be his responsibility. But, dammit, Joel needed to stop running away from his mistakes.

He finally figured out how to get the baby swing folded up to a point it would fit in the trunk of his car.

He hauled it downstairs and then returned for the portable crib. After making several more trips down to the car, he had most of the stuff packed up.

"Is there anything else?" he asked Lacey, watching from the corner of his eye as Elana finished feeding Tucker, holding him on her shoulder and rubbing his back, urging him to burp. Did babies burp on command? He didn't think so. But when Tucker let out a loud belch, he couldn't help but grin.

"I think so," Lacey said hesitantly, wringing her hands together nervously. "Babies sure need a lot of stuff, don't they?"

"You're not kidding," Brock muttered. He forced himself to sound positive. "It's probably good enough for now. We can always come back if you did forget something. And I'm sure Joel will be back soon."

"Yeah. You're probably right," Lacey said in a voice that lacked conviction.

"Do you have the anti-gas medicine?" Elana asked, crossing over to them, still holding the baby.

Lacey's face crumpled. "No. I forgot. And I don't think I packed the formula either."

"Here, Brock." She thrust the baby at him. "Come on, Lacey, let's make one last sweep of the house."

He wanted to protest, but the women disappeared into the kitchen faster than he could blink. Holding his breath, he stared down at his nephew. It wasn't as if he'd never held a baby; infants occasionally ended up in the ED, although not for long since they didn't waste any time transferring them over to Children's Memorial Hospital, located right across the street.

After the accident, he'd refused to contemplate having a family of his own. Children. After stealing Felicity's life, he knew he didn't deserve a family.

Yet he couldn't ignore his nephew. Tucker looked up at him with a solemn, steady gaze. Brock smiled nervously. "Hey, there. You're being a good baby, aren't you? No crying now, and let's try to keep it that way, hmm?"

Tucker blinked and then waved his hands, as if he wanted to say something but obviously couldn't. When Brock put his hand out, the baby grabbed his finger with a surprisingly tight grip.

And when Tucker smiled, the icy reserve around Brock's heart melted into a gooey pile of slush. For the first time, he realized how much he'd given up that day he'd crashed into Felicity's car.

Elana's breath hitched in her chest when she came out of the kitchen and caught sight of the enthralled expression on Brock's face as he gazed down at his nephew.

She tightened her grip on the cans of formula she carried so they didn't slip and crash to the floor.

What was she thinking to react like this? Maybe she could respect Brock's talent as a physician, but she couldn't be attracted to him. Obviously being with him like this outside the hospital was dangerous. It was almost too easy to forget how he'd recklessly killed her sister.

Felicity. She'd idolized her older sister, especially since Felicity had often looked out for Elana when their mother wasn't quite capable. Felicity had been so vibrant, so full of life. Everyone had loved her, Elana most of all.

She drew a ragged breath. *Don't go back. You're a different person now.*

Distance. She needed distance. She needed to get as far away from Brock as possible.

"Do you and Lacey have everything now?" Brock asked.

She put down the cans of formula and curled her fingers into tight fists, the prick of her fingernails helping to sharpen her focus.

"Elana?" he asked again.

"Yes," she croaked. Lacey crossed over to put Tucker into his car seat, giving him his medicine once he was settled in.

"Let's go, then." Brock reached down to pick up the car seat by the handle, holding the door for them so they could head out to the car.

"Put your seat belt on," he said to Lacey after she'd gotten Tucker's car seat fastened.

Elana caught Lacey rolling her eyes, but the young woman didn't protest as she complied with his wishes. Elana had already buckled herself in.

So Brock was fanatical about seat belts. That made sense; working in trauma, you learned the patients who weren't secured in their seat belts, nine times out of ten, suffered more severe injuries than those who complied with the law.

Like Felicity. Chloe had pointed out several times

that her sister might have survived the crash if she had been wearing her seat belt. Her neck had been broken when she'd been ejected from the car.

Brock's fault. It was all Brock's fault.

Wasn't it?

Elana huddled in her seat, her head spinning. She wanted to tell Brock to drop her off first, so she could get away from him, but she should really go to make sure Lacey was settled in before leaving.

She would take a taxi home. Anything to get away from him.

Brock seemed grateful for her help as they proceeded to unpack all the items they'd just stored in the back of his SUV. By the time they had everything set up, it was two o'clock in the morning.

The good news was that Tucker had fallen asleep on the short drive over to Brock's. Brock had carefully carried the sleeping baby inside and set him in the corner of the spare bedroom, where Lacey would also have to sleep.

"That anti-gas medicine really works," Lacey whispered, her gaze full of relief. "If only Joel could see Tucker now, he'd know things weren't so bad."

"Do you think that's why he left?" Elana quietly asked. Brock was still hauling stuff inside while they unpacked.

Lacey nodded. "It was so awful with Tucker crying all the time. Nothing helped. Feeding him, changing his diaper, rocking him, nothing. Joel couldn't take it any more."

Elana tightened her lips, wanting to point out that

Lacey had struggled too but hadn't taken the easy way out by walking away. "Brock will find him, you'll see," she said instead.

"I hope so. I've always been a little afraid of Brock, but he's been nice so far tonight."

Afraid? Elana almost choked out a laugh. She was afraid of Brock too. Of getting close to him. Of not hating him as much as she should. "There's no reason to be afraid," Elana assured her. "I think he's irritated with Joel's disappearing act, but he would never hurt you or Tucker."

"I know. But I still don't think he likes me much," Lacey said, yawning widely, her eyes drooping with exhaustion.

"Get some sleep while Tucker's down," Elana advised. "You'll cope better if you get some rest too. I'll finish putting this stuff away. You can take care of the rest in the morning."

"All right." Lacey offered a shy smile. "Good night, Elana. Thanks for all your help. I don't think I could have done it without you."

Touched, Elana reached over to give Lacey a quick hug. "You're very welcome, Lacey. I'm always available if you need me. Call me any time."

Elana finished setting up the formula, bottles and the medicine along the kitchen counter so that Lacey could easily find them when Tucker woke up hungry in the morning. Brock was still putting the baby swing back together, looking up in surprise when she headed for the door.

"Wait, I'll drive you home," he said, abandoning his project and jumping to his feet.

"No, don't bother. I called a taxi."

He frowned, and she could tell he wasn't happy with her decision. "There's no need to waste your hard-earned money on a taxi," he said testily.

Her sanity was well worth the expense. She edged closer to the door. "It's better for Lacey if you stay here."

He stared at her. "Better for Lacey? Or for you?"

She stopped and squared her shoulders defiantly. "Does it matter?"

"Yes, it does." His voice was soft and compelling. "I never wanted to hurt you, Elana."

"Too late," she whispered. "Good night, Brock." She turned and slipped out the door, overwhelmingly relieved when he didn't follow.

But in the taxi she looked down in surprise at the crimson stains on her fingers. She opened her palms, realizing with a shock that she was bleeding from several spots in her hands where she'd broken the skin with her nails.

Her stomach churned, and for a moment black spots danced before her eyes. She struggled to take a deep breath.

Brock's return was pushing her to the edge of her fragile self-control.

CHAPTER FIVE

BROCK bowed his head, fighting every instinct in his body screaming at him to follow Elana. *Too late*. Her whispered words were seared into his memory. He knew they were true. He was too late. He'd already hurt her.

He stayed where he was, picking up a piece of the swing and continuing to put the various parts back together.

What did his needs matter?

He didn't sleep well; Elana's tortured expression followed him into his dreams. Nightmares. Over the next couple of nights, he lay awake, not falling asleep until the wee hours of the morning, only to be woken up by Tucker's crying.

By the second day, he groaned and shoved his head under the pillow, but it was no use. Logically he knew the little guy was just hungry, and crying was the only way Tucker had to make his needs known. But that shrill tone sent an immediate shock to his system, yanking him out of a deep sleep quicker than any alarm clock.

And then there was Lacey, who tiptoed around him,

jumping like a scared rabbit every time he walked into a room. Tucker still had his colicky crying jags, which only made things worse, as Lacey literally went nuts trying to get him to quiet down. He finally told her to let him cry, which made her break down sobbing herself.

Yeah, Lacey's coping strategies were pretty much non-existent. He kept trying to reassure her that everything would be fine, but after he'd spent his entire day off searching for Joel, without any luck, he found that line hard to believe himself.

When he'd exhausted every contact he had for his brother, Brock was forced to admit Joel had taken off on purpose. This wasn't just a case of his brother needing a break from his seemingly overwhelming responsibilities, getting drunk, overdoing it, and passing out with one of his buddies.

His brother was really gone. As in leaving his girlfriend and infant son to fend for themselves gone.

Or, more likely, leaving without a backward glance because Joel knew Brock would pick up the pieces of his mess and make things right.

To make matters worse, Brock was worried about leaving Lacey home alone with the baby while he went to work Friday night.

He wished he could call Elana; it was obvious to him the two women had bonded the night he'd moved Lacey and Tucker into his house. But Elana didn't want to see him. Or talk to him. Or be anywhere near him.

Clearly, she'd taken a taxi home rather than allowing him to drive her.

So he pulled out the phone book and sat at his kitchen table and made two phone calls. One to a private investigator, hiring a guy named Rufus Kingsley to search for Joel. And the other to a nanny service, hiring a woman to come over to the house while he was gone to help Lacey care for Tucker.

Maybe hiring a nanny was going a bit overboard; Lacey might actually do fine once she stopped freaking out about Tucker's crying disturbing him. But he couldn't help noticing she'd spent a lot of time in the bathroom earlier that morning, and he kept imagining the cuts Elana had seen on Lacey's arm.

He hadn't gotten so much as a glimpse of them himself because Lacey wore those long-sleeved T-shirts that hung all the way down to her bony wrists.

Before he went to work, he went back into the bathroom and stared at the razor over the sink, wondering if it was in the same position where he'd left it or if Lacey had moved it. Muttering under his breath, he took the razor and the blades, hiding them both in his room.

"You hired a nanny?" Lacey asked, staring defiantly at him for the first time since he'd moved her to his house. The nanny in question was standing in the living room, watching them curiously.

Warily he nodded. "Yeah. I thought maybe you could use some time for yourself. To—I don't know—take a bubble bath or go shopping or something."

Lacey stared at him as if he'd told her to strip naked and dance for a room full of old men. "I can take care of Tucker myself."

He suppressed a sigh, glancing at the nanny, a motherly-looking woman whose expression held a note of faint disdain. It had never occurred to him that Lacey would rebel against the idea. "I know you can take care of Tucker yourself. But I'm going to be gone for a long time, and I thought you'd like a little help." And maybe wouldn't feel the need to cut yourself, he silently added.

"Thanks, but I don't need any help." Lacey stoutly crossed her arms over her chest.

Brock wavered, inwardly debating. He didn't have time for an argument. If he didn't leave soon, he'd be late for work. The stubborn expression on Lacey's face forced him to cave in to her wishes, against his better judgment.

"All right," he said, hoping he wasn't making a mistake in trusting her. "If you're sure."

"I'm sure."

He turned to the nanny and pulled out his wallet. "I'll pay for the day, but you're not needed here after all. Thanks anyway."

"Hrumph," she said, clear disproval etched on her features as she hitched her purse on her shoulder and took the cash he offered. "I guess you can call me again if the situation changes."

Lacey glowered at the woman, her gaze clearly saying the situation would not change in her lifetime, leaving Brock to escort the woman out of the house. He glanced back at Lacey. "I'll be at work if you need me."

She nodded. "We'll be fine."

He hoped so. He carried enough guilt; he didn't need something bad happening to Lacey on top of everything else. Closing the door behind him, he hurried to his car, ducking his head against the April showers pouring from the sky and pounding the pavement.

The gloomy weather matched his mood. Lacey was likely relieved to have him out of the way, and Elana was no doubt dreading working with him. There wasn't much he could do about the latter, other than try to stay out of Elana's way.

And hope that it was enough.

Elana cursed her luck when she discovered she'd been assigned to work in the trauma bay with Brock. She'd asked for her assignment to be changed, but there were no other trauma-trained nurses working in the arena for her to switch with. Nurses had to work in the arena for at least a year before they could be trained in trauma.

In the past few days, she'd been happy with the reprieve of seeing Brock. She'd vowed not to let him drag her back down into the depths of despair. That night in the taxi, when she'd noticed her blood-stained fingers, she'd realized how close she'd been to losing it.

The very next morning, she'd stopped in at the human resources department to formally request a transfer to the critical care unit. She'd been hoping that they'd take her right away, but she was told she needed to wait for the manager to call.

That was some days ago, and still she hadn't gotten a call. Now she had to work with Brock again. At least it was Friday night, one of the busiest nights of the week, so there wouldn't be a lot of down time.

Brock walked into the trauma bay, deep grooves of exhaustion lining his face, and immediately her thoughts went to Lacey and Tucker. Where they doing all right? Or had something happened?

Surely he'd come and tell her if something was wrong with Lacey or Tucker. Wouldn't he?

Working with Brock wasn't nearly as bad as she'd feared. His leadership style was more collegial than not. If she didn't think about it too much, she could forget her animosity towards him and fall into a synchronized rhythm. And when two patients arrived, sporting identical gunshot wounds, it was a good thing she could anticipate exactly what he needed.

"Give me the latest set of vitals, Elana," he said when she'd completed her assessment.

"BP 88/42, pulse tachy at 118. Respirations up a bit at 30, but not labored." She glanced up at the IVs, not having the luxury of Raine's help as she was busy in the other trauma bay with her own patient, and Brock was going back and forth, leading both resuscitations at the same time. "Do you want more fluids? Or blood products?"

"Blood products," Brock announced. "Keep the left PIV running with normal saline, but start with one unit of O-negative packed cells on the right until we get the lab results back. The bullet is still lodged somewhere in his belly; the trauma surgeon on call should be here soon."

"Got it," Elana said, having already reached for the unit of packed red blood cells. She automatically drew a full set of labs once she'd hung the blood, keeping an eye on the patient's bedside monitor as she handed the tubes of blood to the ED tech.

Their side-by-side gunshot victims were soon dispatched upstairs, one to the OR for surgery, the other to the ICU to wait for his turn in the OR, since both penetrating wounds were serious but not immediately life-threatening. The worst part came when the respective family members of the victims began arguing loudly, escalating into a full-blown physical altercation in the waiting room.

Once the cops had hauled the offenders away, each side blaming the other for starting the fight, things quickly settled back to normal.

"Takes all kinds," Brock muttered under his breath.

"You're not kidding," Elana couldn't help but agree.

His sizzling blue gaze clung to hers, making her breath catch in her throat. For a moment it felt as if they were the only two people alone in the entire department. She took a hasty step back. Professionalism was one thing, but allowing Brock to get too close was something completely different.

The light in Brock's eyes dimmed when she turned away, and she was hit by an unexpected pang of regret. If things had been different, maybe…

No. Don't go there.

Thankfully the trauma pager went off, announcing another arrival. Soon afterwards, they received another one. The trauma bay was hopping, but they were able to move patients through the system pretty well.

Towards the end of their shift, they got a call about a

young eighteen-year-old patient who'd overdosed on wine and pain pills found in her mother's medicine cabinet.

"Didn't her mother listen to those commercials warning parents to lock up their prescription meds?" Raine plaintively asked in a low tone to Elana.

"I guess not." Elana took her place on the right side of the patient, gasping when she saw the young woman carried a slight resemblance to Lacey.

"Get a nasogastric tube down her, stat," Brock ordered. "Get the activated charcoal ready to go."

Elana did her assessment while Raine prepared to place the tube. "Her pupils are dilated and very sluggish. She's not responsive to verbal stimuli or pain. BP low at 78/40."

"We need a full toxicology screen, Elana. We don't know if she took more than the empty bottle of painkillers that her mother found on the floor next to her."

Brock's terse tone convinced her that he'd noticed the slight resemblance to Lacey too. Elana could only imagine how depressed this young woman must have been to take such drastic steps. Or maybe it was simply a cry for help.

A silent plea that could end in disaster.

Raine passed the nasogastric tube down into the girl's stomach, pumping the first diluted bottle of activated charcoal through the tube as quickly as possible.

Once she'd sent the tox screen, Elana helped Raine with the mess. Because shortly after the first contents hit their patient's stomach, the girl began retching violently.

"It's okay, Ariel. We're going to get that poison out of your system," Elana said, smoothing the girl's limp blonde hair away from her face. "You're going to be okay."

Ariel Peterson cried between bouts of retching. Elana didn't mind the mess so much; having Ariel crying and throwing up was better than having her comatose from the drugs.

"Here's the results of the tox screen," the tech said, handing her the slip of paper from the lab.

"Nothing more than the narcotic and the alcohol, and those levels aren't as bad as they could be," Elana announced, catching Brock's gaze. "Her mother found her early enough."

"Thank God," he muttered. "I'm going to arrange an ICU bed for her. We can hold off with the next dose of charcoal as long as she stays responsive."

Elana nodded, relieved to know Ariel would survive after all.

She and Raine transferred Ariel to the ICU. Miraculously, Elana had come out of the resuscitation without a single charcoal stain. Raine hadn't been quite so lucky.

"Next time, I'm taking the right side of an overdose patient," Raine muttered darkly, grimacing at the black streaks running down the side of her leg.

"Hey, at least it's the end of our shift," Elana pointed out. "Could be worse. Give me your trauma pager, and then you can grab a new pair of scrubs before you head home."

"Don't worry, I will." Raine handed off her pager and veered off towards the OR locker rooms. "See you later."

Elana lifted a hand and hurried back downstairs. She gave a brief report and handed off the two trauma pagers to the on-coming night-shift nurses. When she walked into the staff lounge, she saw Brock was on his cell phone.

"I'm glad the baby is doing better, Lacey. Get some sleep. I'll see you in the morning."

Lacey? She'd been about to leave, but concern over Lacey and Tucker had her walking further into the room. "Is everything all right with Lacey?" she asked once he'd hung up his phone.

"Yeah. I guess." He let out a heavy sigh. "Seeing Ariel gave me a sick feeling about Lacey, but she swears she's fine."

"I know, I have to admit I worried about the same thing," Elana admitted. "I'm glad to hear things are going better."

"I tried to hire a nanny to stay with her while I'm at work, but Lacey freaked."

A nanny? He really didn't understand women at all. She raised a brow. "Generous of you, but I'm not surprised. I'm sure she took that move as proof you don't trust her to be alone with the baby."

"What am I supposed to do?" Brock asked in a vexed tone. "I had to hide my razors, for God's sake."

"But Lacey wouldn't hurt Tucker," she reminded him gently. "She's only been hurting herself."

"Maybe. But I didn't want to take any chances."

She couldn't blame him for being worried. Self-mutilation could easily escalate into something more. She veered away from those dark thoughts. "I take it you haven't found Joel yet?"

"No." Brock sank into a chair, his shoulders slumping

in defeat. "I spent my entire day off yesterday looking for him, but no luck. I ended up hiring a private investigator to find him."

Wow. It seemed he'd been busy. And concerned. No wonder he'd looked so exhausted earlier. As much as she wanted to avoid him, she realized she couldn't walk away. Hesitantly she took a seat across from him. "You can't force him to be a father."

"I know. But it's not fair for Lacey and Tucker to suffer either."

He was right. She couldn't argue that one.

"Lacey keeps telling me that Tucker is better, that he's not crying as much, but I think she's fooling herself," Brock continued. "He really is colicky; the poor kid cried for nearly an hour straight before he finally fell asleep in his swing." He raised his resigned gaze to hers. "I'm worried about her."

"Lacey isn't going to end up like Ariel," she said softly. "We won't let her."

"We?" Brock arched a brow. "You've done more than enough, Elana. Lacey and Tucker are not your problem, they're mine."

"She was my patient in the clinic," she reminded him. She didn't add how much Lacey reminded Elana of herself at that age. Chloe had saved her, but who was going to save Lacey? Elana wasn't sure Brock even understood what the poor girl needed. His trying to hire a nanny was proof of that.

No, she refused to abandon Lacey.

"Lacey trusts me. I'd like to help."

"You already have been a huge help to her," Brock agreed. "I owe you for that. I guess I can understand why Lacey finds it easier to talk to you than to me."

"I don't mind."

There was a moment of companionable silence. The animosity she normally felt toward Brock seemed to have vanished. She was amazed at how easy it was to discuss Lacey's issues.

Much easier than discussing her own thoughts and feelings, that was for sure.

"I guess I should get going," she murmured, feeling a little like the traitor who'd consorted with the enemy. She rose to her feet and headed for the door.

"Elana?" Brock's voice stopped her.

"Yes?" She turned back towards him.

"Thank you. I know I don't deserve your kindness, but I want you to know how much I appreciate your help."

She shrugged, shaken by his sincere gratitude. He seemed so different from the man she'd hated for all those years after Felicity's death.

"If I ask you a question, will you tell me the truth?" she asked.

His eyes widened in surprise. "Of course," he said gruffly.

She gathered her courage. "There were rumors about you speeding that night," she said in a rush before she could change her mind. "That your father, the cop, covered for you so you wouldn't go to jail."

She didn't have to explain what night she was talking about: he knew. "I wasn't. I swear to you, Elana,

I wasn't speeding. If you knew my father, you'd understand the last thing he'd ever do is cover up for me."

She hesitated, wishing she could believe him. "No matter how difficult your relationship with your father, I'm sure he wouldn't be so cold as to put you in jail."

He let out a harsh laugh. "Don't bet on it. Elana, do you know why I had to move back home to Milwaukee?" When she shook her head, he continued. "Because my father lashed out at Joel after he got Lacey pregnant. Our old man basically threw him out onto the street with nothing but the clothes on his back. Joel called me in a panic because the cheapest apartment he could afford didn't allow kids. I came home because my father refused to give him a dime."

Elana didn't know what to say. The stark statement rang true.

"I wasn't speeding, Elana. But I also know that there's nothing I can say to make up for what happened. You have no idea how much that night has haunted me."

Yes, she did. Because that night haunted her too.

"I tried to save her. I had a broken clavicle—the bone was poking right out of the skin—but I still did CPR at the scene until help arrived. The image of your sister's face will be ingrained in my mind for the rest of my life."

Tears burned in her eyes, her throat clogged with regret. She'd loved her sister. Yet it was just as clear that Brock hadn't escaped unscathed. He looked at her expectantly, but she couldn't say the words he wanted to hear.

I forgive you.

Blindly she turned away, but Brock was there, grasping her hand to stop her.

"Don't cry, Elana," he said in a low, husky voice. "Please don't cry."

When he reached up to wipe her tears away, her breath caught in her throat. The brush of his fingers against her skin was like an electrical shock, sending a tingling wave of awareness dancing down her spine.

He was close. Too close. The male scent of him, a hint of aftershave mixed with honest sweat, enveloped her. For long moments they stared deeply into each other's eyes, as if held by an invisible string that was slowly tightening, drawing them together.

She was shocked by the abrupt desire to throw herself into his arms, seeking comfort.

"I have to go," she said in a strangled whisper, breaking out of his grasp. As she hurried away, she could feel his intense gaze boring into her back.

And it took every ounce of willpower to keep on walking.

CHAPTER SIX

BROCK took several deep breaths, realizing he'd nearly crossed the line with Elana, big-time. He'd wanted nothing more than to pull her into his arms. Would have offered her comfort and anything else she'd needed.

Shaky, as if he'd shot-gunned a six-pack of the highest octane energy drink, he scrubbed his hands over his face. The enticing vanilla scent of her lingered in the air, messing with his head.

It was crazy. Completely insane. But there was no point in lying to himself.

He wanted more than her forgiveness.

He wanted her.

Even knowing how much she hated him, would do anything to avoid being with him, he still wanted her.

Pathetic. Self-destructive. Hopeless. He shook his head at his own foolishness.

All this time she'd thought he was speeding the night her sister had pulled out in front of him. No wonder she'd been so upset. He clearly remembered the insults she'd screamed at him when he'd shown up at Felicity's funeral. Now he understood a little better why she'd been so angry.

He'd told Elana the truth. He hadn't been speeding. But he had no way of knowing if she believed him or not.

And even if she did, what did it matter? The end result was the same. She wouldn't forgive him. Hell, he didn't forgive himself.

He'd thrown himself into his work, sacrificing his personal life to save others. Trying to make up for losing Felicity.

So why was he longing for a relationship now? With the one woman he could never have? He needed to stay away from Elana, now more than ever. For one thing, he wasn't sure he could trust himself around her: his body didn't listen to logic. And there was always the extremely remote possibility that if she ever did want more from him, he'd succumb. He'd never deny her.

Which would be bad since his track record with women sucked. He'd indulged in the occasional one-night stand, hating himself afterwards. Elana deserved someone better. Someone who could offer her a life. A future. He needed to get the turmoil of wanting Elana out of his head, and fast.

Before he managed to hurt her all over again.

The next morning, Brock dragged himself out of bed early because Tucker was crying louder and longer than usual.

Yeah, the kid had colic, but even after a few days with his nephew, Brock could tell the difference between his colicky cry and this sharper, desperate one.

Bleary-eyed, he shuffled into the kitchen, searching for coffee. Lacey jumped when he walked in, spilling her cup of tea. As she hurried to wipe up the mess, he squelched the urge to apologize for walking through his own house, trying to smile at her reassuringly. "Hey, Lacey. Seems like Tucker's having a rough morning."

The baby was propped in his infant seat on top of the kitchen table. Her face immediately crumpled. "I don't know what's wrong with him," she wailed brokenly. "I carried him around for an hour, tried feeding him and changing him. I just don't know what's wrong."

"Hey, it's okay. You're a great mom, honest. This isn't your fault. Here, I'll take a look at him, okay?" He made a rash promise, forgoing the need for coffee as he unhooked Tucker from his seat and lifted him in his arms. "We can always take him back to the clinic too if needed."

"Okay." Her puffy, reddened eyes filled with hope. Not good, since he was hardly a miracle worker: there was no magic touch to make the baby stop crying.

Tucker didn't quiet down for him either, the wailing much louder with the baby on his shoulder, close to his ear. Tucker felt warm, his nose and throat far more congested than they'd been a few days ago. Carrying Tucker into his bedroom, Brock fished out his stethoscope, wishing he owned a pediatric ophthalmoscope.

Setting Tucker on his bed, he did his best to examine him with the limited equipment he had. He'd bet Tucker's ears were red and inflamed, but he couldn't prove it since he didn't have a pediatric scope. The baby's lungs definitely sounded a bit congested too.

He doubted Lacey had given Tucker any over-the-counter medication but Brock thought the baby could benefit from getting a decongestant into his system. Tucker also seemed to be a bit dehydrated.

"We need to take him back to the clinic," he told Lacey, bringing Tucker back into the kitchen. "He might have an ear infection, and, if so, he'll need a course of antibiotics."

"All right." She reached up for the baby, the sleeve of her right arm sliding up a bit to reveal two thin cuts on her forearm, somewhat scabbed over but still looking fairly recent.

He froze.

Should he call Elana? He wanted to. He felt out of his depth with Lacey's cutting behavior. Yet was this bad enough to bother Elana with on a Saturday? After all, Lacey's cuts weren't bleeding or anything. At least not the ones he'd caught a glimpse of. He'd almost pulled out his phone before he realized he didn't have Elana's number. He'd have to call the ED to get it.

Tempted, he hesitated. He forced himself to think rationally. Did he want to call Elana for Lacey's sake? Or for his own?

To make himself feel better. Disturbed, he stuck the phone back in his pocket and handed Lacey the baby. He fetched his wallet and car keys as Lacey put Tucker into his infant carrier.

He could handle this crisis without Elana's help. He

drove to the New Beginnings Clinic, telling himself that leaving Elana out of his problems was the right thing to do. He could always mention the cuts on Lacey's arm the next time he saw her at work.

The clinic was packed, and he did his best to wait patiently in line until it was their turn, even though he wanted to march in there, demanding Tucker be seen next.

"Lacey and Tucker?" the petite receptionist called out. "You're next. Follow me."

Surprised that they were taken so quickly, although it was possible the receptionist behind the desk couldn't take Tucker's crying any more than he could, he gratefully followed Lacey and the baby into the tiny exam room.

A nurse turned to face them when they came in.

His jaw dropped to his chest in surprise when he saw Elana.

"Lacey!" Elana looked just as surprised to see them. Her gaze skittered over him and landed on Lacey and Tucker. She frowned. "What's wrong?"

"Tucker's crying again, but it's different this time, Elana." Lacey shocked him by speaking up for herself. "Honest, it's not the same colicky cry as before."

Brock felt the need to stick up for Lacey. "She's right, you can definitely tell the difference."

"I believe you, Lacey," Elana assured her, barely glancing at him.

"I examined him at home, but I didn't have a pediatric ophthalmoscope," Brock explained. "So I couldn't look at his ears. The way he's acting, though, I'm betting he has bilateral ear infections."

This time, she didn't ignore him. "Thanks, Brock. I'll take a quick look, and then I'll get Dr Liz in here right away."

Feeling unusually useless—normally he was the one in charge within a medical situation—he stepped back and tucked his hands into the pockets of his jeans. Elana was focused on Tucker, using the pediatric ophthalmoscope to peer into his ears. With her silky dark hair pulled back into a ponytail, he found it difficult to tear his gaze away from the graceful curve of her neck.

"Brock's right," Elana murmured a few minutes later. "Hold on to Tucker, Lacey, while I get Dr Liz."

Dr Liz Jacoby was a statuesque woman who took charge the minute she entered the room. Impressed with her gentle, yet no-nonsense manner, he was pleased when she quickly concurred with his diagnosis.

"This little guy needs a full course of antibiotics," she announced. "Good thing you brought him in when you did."

"Maybe I should have taken him straight to Trinity Medical Center's ED, where I work. I'm Dr Brock Madison," he introduced himself belatedly.

"Personally, I'm glad you came here." Liz's wide gaze sharpened on him. "You're the new guy, aren't you? Recruited from Minneapolis? I've heard you're a good addition to the emergency department team." Liz Jacoby flashed a brilliantly white smile. "So what do you think of my little clinic, hmm? If you're interested, we're always looking for new doctors to volunteer their time."

There was a loud crash as Elana dropped a tray of instruments she'd been carrying to the sink. He couldn't help but notice the flash of horror on her face. Obviously, Elana didn't want him anywhere near the clinic.

"I'll think about it," he hedged, unwilling to flat-out refuse when he knew that clinics like this depended on volunteers to stay afloat. "At the moment, I'm pretty busy helping Lacey and Tucker."

Liz frowned, casting a quick glance at Elana, who had knelt to pick up the instruments from the floor. "I understand, but it's an open invitation if anything changes. Even one or two shifts a month would help."

"Sure thing," he said, unable to refuse.

Elana took the tray to the sink, her back stiff, radiating disapproval.

Liz handed him the prescription for Tucker's antibiotics.

"Thanks," he murmured.

They were making their way out of the exam room when Raine rushed in.

"Thanks for covering for me, Elana. See, I told you I'd be here in plenty of time for you to go visit your mom at the nursing home."

Visit her mother? Brock ushered Lacey and Tucker toward the lobby, stealing a quick glance back at Elana. He wished he had the time to reassure her he wouldn't volunteer at the New Beginnings Clinic if she didn't want him to. But she was busy talking to Raine, and Tucker needed his medicine sooner rather than later, so he left.

He wondered if Elana's mother was still in the same nursing home as she had been eight and a half years ago. Chances were good she was.

When Lacey mentioned she needed more soy-based formula, Brock headed to the nearest pharmacy instead of going to the hospital for cheaper antibiotics. As they waited for the script to be filled, he decided it would be best to stock up on some needed supplies. Rehydration solutions to help keep Tucker hydrated, lung decongestant medicine, a case of soy-based formula, a pack of diapers and, last but not least, the antibiotics.

Eighty-three dollars and ninety-six cents later, he grimly acknowledged that caring for an infant was far more expensive than he'd ever realized, and the antibiotics were the cheapest item in the cart.

No wonder Joel had felt overwhelmed.

The New Beginnings Clinic offering free medical care was only a drop in the bucket of what a new mother needed to provide for a baby.

He wished he could help at the clinic. But he wouldn't risk causing Elana any more distress. Surely there was some other way he could donate his time. Some cause that would still benefit people like Lacey and Tucker.

Brock dropped Lacey and Tucker off at home, making sure they had everything they needed. He reinforced with Lacey that the liquid antibiotic needed to be kept in the refrigerator between doses.

Glancing at his watch, he decided he had a couple of hours before he needed to get to the hospital for his shift. Before he fully realized his intent, he found himself heading for the Cottage Grove Nursing Home.

He'd hang around outside until Elana finished visiting with her mother. Surely she'd feel better once he'd convinced her he had no intention of encroaching on her work at the clinic.

No matter how much it pained him, he'd promise to stay out of her way from this point forward.

Elana bypassed her usual stop at the nurses' station for an update though her mother's condition rarely changed. Outside her mother's room, she took a deep breath and pasted a cheery smile on her face to buoy her spirits before walking in.

The aides had gotten her mother up out of bed and seated in her rocking chair by the window. They'd also taken pains to dress her up in her favorite bright pink housecoat in honor of Elana's visit.

"Hi, Mom, it's so good to see you." Elana crossed over to give her mother a hug and kiss before taking a seat beside her. She took her mother's hand in hers and captured her mother's gaze. "How have you been? Are they still taking good care of you here?"

Her mother held her gaze and tightened her grip twice in their communication code. One squeeze meant no but two squeezes meant yes. Her mother's emotional status had been extremely fragile: her first nervous breakdown had occurred right after their father had taken off. After Felicity's death, her mother had retreated further, hiding from everything painful in a world of silence.

The doctors had been wonderful; they'd made a little progress over the years, getting her mother to make eye contact and respond to verbal commands, but the process seemed to go so slowly.

She longed to hear her mother's voice.

"I'm glad things are going good, Mom." She forced herself to sound cheerful. "You know, I think it's time to get you some new pictures. These prints have been up for almost three months now. Well past time for a change in scenery."

Her mother glanced at the splashy, colorful prints Elana had put up on the wall, but then turned away. Her mother's fingers tightened around hers once. No.

"Come on, Mom. You love art, remember?" Elana imagined her mother was feeling as if she shouldn't bother, but, in reality, buying new pictures for her mother made Elana feel as if she were doing something, even if it was something as simple as buying new prints. The medical staff had used art therapy to encourage her mother to stay connected to the world. So far, her mother had made several watercolor paintings, so she liked to think the new therapy was working.

Her mother looked away, and Elana wished she knew what was going on in her mother's mind. Carrying on yes-and-no conversations were heart-wrenchingly difficult.

"Don't you think new pictures would be a nice change?"

After what seemed like forever, her mother squeezed her hand twice. Yes. Elana relaxed, hoping this was a sign of more progress.

She went through her usual conversation tidbits, telling her mother about her work at the clinic and some of her patients, keeping the stories as upbeat as possible. Her mother answered the occasional question with yes or no hand squeezes.

When she ran out of chatty things to say, she stared at her mother's hand in hers. It was at times like this she missed her mother the most. When she needed a confidant.

She winced at her selfish thought. Her mother's emotional health had been fragile for years; it wasn't her mother's fault she had difficulty coping with the added stress of her sister's death.

"I met Brock Madison," she finally said in a low voice, hoping and praying her mother wouldn't react negatively to Brock's name. "Do you remember him?"

She risked a glance at her mother's face. Her mother's gaze was clear, alert. She squeezed her fingers twice. Yes.

Elana was surprised her mother didn't appear to be upset. Was this a good sign? Maybe that art therapy was working better than she'd imagined.

"He claims he wasn't speeding that night," Elana continued, needing to get some of this inner turmoil out of her system. "He said the last thing his dad would do is to cover up for him, and I think I'm starting to believe him. Did you know he's a doctor now?"

One squeeze. No, her mother hadn't known Brock was a doctor. Encouraged by the intensity of her mother's gaze, and feeling as if they were actually having a mean-ingful conversation, she continued.

"We work together in the emergency department. He's a really good doctor. He gives everything he has to save his patients."

Her mother's gaze clung to hers, and Elana had the sense her mother wanted to say something. She waited a few minutes, but the words remained locked deep inside.

Nervously she licked her lips. "I don't know what to think, Mom. I know everything is his fault, yet I can't seem to hate him as much as I used to."

"Life's short," her mother suddenly rasped. "Hate isn't worth it."

Elana sucked in a shocked breath, her eyes stinging with tears. She'd spoken! Her mother had actually spoken! She struggled not to make too much of a big deal of the event, even though she wanted to dance around the room, screaming with joy.

"I know life is too short, Mom. You're right—wasting time on negative energy doesn't help anyone." She reached over to engulf her mother in a tight hug. "I love you, Mom. I love you so much."

"Love you, Elana," her mother whispered.

Elana's eyes welled with tears again. Things were going to be fine. She just knew it.

And she couldn't help wondering if her mother's breakthrough had something to do with her confessions about Brock. This was the first time she'd ever really opened up about her thoughts and fears.

Maybe she should have confided in her mother sooner.

"I have to go to work, Mom," she said regretfully when she'd stayed as long as she dared. "But I'll be back soon, I promise."

Her mother squeezed her hand twice, and Elana hoped and prayed that now that her mother had spoken, she'd only continue to improve.

She held her emotions in check long enough to update the nurses, who promised to let the doctor know. Yet she couldn't help feeling guilty, as if she could have impacted her mother's health sooner if she'd only opened up to her.

Her throat swelled with tears, and suddenly she couldn't stay in the nursing home for another second. She flew towards the door, throwing it wide open in her haste to get outside.

And barreled straight into Brock's arms.

"Elana?" Brock caught her close, preventing her from taking a header into the concrete sidewalk, his expression full of alarm. "What is it? What's wrong?"

"Nothing! Leave me alone. I'm fine!" She twisted, trying to break away, but he was much stronger and only tightened his grip.

"You're not fine. You're crying. Tell me what's wrong."

"Good tears," she whispered, trying to swipe them away in an attempt to get a hold of herself, but the sobs in her chest struggled to break loose. "She spoke! After all these years, my mother finally spoke!"

Despite the fact that she considered Brock the enemy, she collapsed against him, burying her face against his chest and letting go, crying as if she might never stop.

CHAPTER SEVEN

BROCK held Elana close, inwardly reeling at the news. Her mother had spoken? It sounded like good news, but the way she continued to cry worried him. He could feel dampness on his shirt from the force of her tears. He closed his eyes, the familiar snake of guilt uncoiling in his gut, twisting and turning.

Her mother might be improving, but he couldn't ignore the fact that his actions had caused her mother to withdraw from the world in the first place.

Yet another reason for Elana to hate him.

He didn't for one minute believe Elana had forgiven him just because she'd broken down crying in his arms. Especially when, all too soon, the maelstrom of her tears subsided, and she broke away, furiously swiping at her face.

"Sorry about the waterworks," she muttered, sniffling loudly and digging in her purse for a tissue. "I don't know what's wrong with me."

"Don't." He realised his tone must have been sharper than he'd intended when her shocked gaze snapped up to his. "You have nothing to apologize for," he said, trying to soften the edge of his tone. "Nothing."

She stared at him for a long minute, then pulled out a tissue and blew her nose. Hard.

Hating the feeling of helplessness, he glanced back toward the Cottage Grove Nursing Home. "She's really talking?"

Elana's tremulous smile broke his heart. "Well, she said a few words. But I think it's a sign she's finally healing."

He hoped so too, more than Elana could ever know. He was afraid to hope, but tried to remain positive. Elana was happy, which was all that mattered.

"What are you doing here?" she asked, glancing around as if surprised to realize they were still standing on the sidewalk outside the nursing home.

"I came to see you."

"Me? Why?" Now her gaze was full of narrow suspicion. Their moment of brief closeness faded. "Can't you just leave me alone?"

Her frank annoyance bothered him. "Yes. That's exactly why I came to find you. I wanted to ease your mind about Dr Liz's offer. I have no intention of volunteering my time at the New Beginnings Clinic."

"Sure, make me be the bad guy with Dr Liz." Elana's gaze filled with disgust. "She needs doctors like you more than nurses like me."

He let out a frustrated breath. "So what are you saying? You want me to take her up on the offer?"

"Doesn't matter to me." She gave an unconvincing careless shrug. "We won't be working together much longer. I'm transferring to a position in the ICU as soon as it's available."

"No!" The vehement protest slipped out before he could stop it. "Don't leave trauma nursing." *Not because of me.*

She glanced away as if she could barely stand the idea of leaving the ED herself. "I have to go. I'm working second shift tonight, and I'm already running late."

So was he. Knowing he'd see her in less than an hour gave him the strength to step back. Hadn't he promised to stay away? "Are you sure you're okay? Maybe I should drive you home."

"I'm fine. My mother is on the road to recovery, so I'm happy." She did look better; there was a rosy flush to her cheeks that had been missing earlier. "Goodbye, Brock."

"Take care of yourself, Elana."

He watched her as she walked away, heading back across the street and into the parking lot where she'd left her car. He knew giving Elana the distance she craved was the right thing to do. She seemed thrilled about her mother's progress, yet she was still angry with him.

He was beginning to realize Elana would never heal from her emotional scars. Not until she put the past behind her once and for all.

Elana worked very hard, without much success, to shake off the rippling effect of that momentary madness in Brock's arms.

What was wrong with her? Why did she seem to be unequivocally drawn to the one man who was absolutely wrong for her? Why couldn't she figure out a way to pry him out of her life once and for all?

Despite her shower, the unique scent of him, musky male intermixed with soap, clouded her senses. When he'd cradled her in his arms, it had been all too easy to forget who he really was.

She didn't want to admit she was hopelessly infatuated with the enemy.

When she walked into the arena, he was standing in front of the census board, talking to a nurse named Eric. He didn't glance at her as she went past.

Assuming Brock was assigned to the arena, she was relieved to learn she'd been assigned to the trauma bay again. Telling Brock her plans of moving to the ICU had backfired. His plea for her not to go still echoed in her mind. He was right: she did love trauma nursing. Yet she was just as certain she'd learn to love critical care too.

Raine had the day off, leaving Eric Towne as her partner in trauma for the shift.

There was still a patient in the trauma bay waiting to be transferred to the ICU. An elderly woman, who was intubated and on a ventilator as a result of contracting tetanus.

"I don't understand," her husband said, obviously stressed out over the seriousness of his wife's illness. "I thought tetanus wasn't a problem any more. That people didn't get lockjaw like they used to."

"They don't if you continue to get your tetanus booster shots every ten years," Dr Laurel Carmen said gently. "Your wife loves to garden, but you said yourself she sustained a severe cut on her finger a few weeks ago. She didn't come in for a tetanus shot and hasn't had one in almost twenty years."

The elderly man's shoulders slumped. "I should have made her come in," he murmured. "But it was just a small cut."

Elana approached Dani, the day shift nurse who was caring for Mrs James, their tetanus patient. "Is there something I can do to help you get her transferred upstairs?" she asked.

"I have everything caught up; we're just waiting for a bed."

"I'll see what I can do." Elana went to the nearest phone, calling up to the medical ICU to find out how much longer before they'd get a bed.

"Housekeeping is in there right now cleaning it," the ICU nurse informed her. "Why don't you give me report? By the time we're done, she should be finished with the room."

"Okay, hang on a minute." Elana called Dani over and handed her the phone. "They're asking for report. You can leave when you're finished; I'll get Mrs James packed up and transported upstairs."

"Thanks," Dani said gratefully.

The trauma bay remained busy with a steady stream of patients, not too surprising for a Saturday night. She was upset to discover Brock was moved into the trauma bay to help with the strong influx of patients. Being so close to him in the confined space was difficult. If she didn't know better, she'd think he was following her on purpose.

Yet she couldn't deny he'd come out to her mother's nursing home just to let her know he wouldn't volunteer at the New Beginnings Clinic. Because she'd betrayed her true feelings by dropping that tray of instruments on the floor when Dr Liz had tried recruiting him.

He was tormenting her with his kindness and understanding. She wasn't sure how much more she could take.

The awkwardness between her and Brock grew more noticeable the harder they tried to stay out of each other's way.

She reached for the patient's clipboard at the same time he did. A tingly awareness shot up her arm as their fingers touched.

She snatched hers back quickly, avoiding his gaze.

"Get me a chest X-ray stat," Brock said tersely. "I have a bad feeling about this guy's abdominal pain."

Elana hurried to carry out his orders, wondering what diagnosis he was considering but not brave enough to ask.

"What are you thinking?" Eric asked, as if reading her mind. "Hot gall bladder? Or appendicitis?"

"Neither. Possible abdominal aortic aneurysm. We need to get him to surgery asap before it dissects."

Why he couldn't have told them that from the beginning, she wasn't sure, but Elana wasted no time in getting the requested X-rays. And after the films were done, and the diagnosis confirmed, Brock continued to give orders.

"Keep his blood pressure under control with the labetalol. I don't want to see anything higher than 120 systolic, understand?"

She nodded, noticing how he avoided speaking her name. She missed the camaraderie they had the other day.

Before she'd collapsed like a weeping willow in his arms.

The surgeons came down to evaluate Roger Ames, their abdominal aortic aneurysm patient, and soon they were getting him ready for the operating room. His aneurysm hadn't dissected yet, but time was of the essence. Ruptured aneurysms had a very poor survival rate.

When their patient was safely in the OR, she helped Eric clean up the mess, putting things away and restocking the supplies. Brock left to briefly talk to Roger's family, letting the wife know her husband was heading to surgery.

"Eric, how are your twin boys doing?" she asked, hoping to use her colleague to break the stilted silence that hovered when Brock returned to the trauma bay.

"The terrors of Towne?" he joked. "They're great. Although Mandy is ready to pull her hair out now that they're three and have discovered the word NO. It's their favorite word, by the way. Between the two of them I bet they say no a hundred times a day."

She had to laugh. She noticed that Brock was listening to their light conversation, a slight grin on his face, although he remained silent, not joining in. "The terrible threes are something, aren't they?"

"You're not kidding. Mandy's been threatening to go back to work, leaving me to stay home with them until they're in school." Eric's wife was a respiratory therapist, but she'd only worked one day a week since the twins were born.

She was about to say something about Tucker, to bring Brock into the conversation, but he interrupted before she could say a word.

"I'm going to the arena. Call if you need me." Brock headed towards the door.

She watched him, telling herself this was what she'd wanted, to be left alone. So why did she want very badly to follow him? Because she was a glutton for punishment?

"What is up with you and Doc Madison?" Eric asked.

She scowled, swinging around to face him. "Have you been talking to Raine?"

"No!" Eric raised his hands up in surrender. "But seriously, Elana, the tension radiates between you guys like we're standing in the middle of a nuclear power plant. So what gives?"

"Nothing." Okay, so maybe that was a lie, but she wasn't about to blab about her personal life to her colleague.

"Fine." Eric seemed annoyed. "If you want to pretend nothing is wrong then, hey, go ahead. Don't let me be the one to burst your bubble."

With a sigh, she lifted a hand to massage the tight muscles in the back of her neck, knowing Eric was right. Things had been tense with Brock, and pretending everything was fine wasn't helping.

She needed to get away. She needed that transfer to the ICU. Maybe she could ask her boss to help get the wheels moving on that paperwork so the process would go a little faster. Surely it would be easier to forget about Brock when she wasn't seeing him every day.

At that moment their pagers went off, announcing a new arrival, effectively bringing their personal conversation to an end.

The message on their pagers read:

Twenty-two-year-old male pedestrian struck by a car, BP 62/30, pulse 144 and irregular, coded once and intubated in the field.

Didn't sound promising. Brock must have gotten the page too, since he joined them in the trauma bay a few minutes later, his expression grim.

When the ambulance doors burst open, she noticed their patient was covered in blood from head to toe, bleeding from various sites. In the battle between pedestrians and vehicles, the pedestrians were often the losers. From the very beginning, Elana knew this patient's outcome wasn't going to be much different.

But Brock was just as determined to do everything possible to prolong the inevitable outcome.

"Eric, get more plasma and blood running now," he snapped. "Elana, I need a chest tube tray: he's bleeding into his lungs."

She nodded, setting the chest tube tray on the over-bed table, opening the tray while keeping the contents inside sterile. Brock expertly inserted the chest tube, and almost instantly blood poured through the clear tubing, filling the plastic receptacle at an alarming pace.

"His pressure is dropping, only fifty-four systolic," Elana said.

"Get more blood. I want four units on the rapid infuser at all times," Brock ordered. "Get me the thoracic surgery team stat. This kid needs the OR."

She briefly met Eric's gaze, both silently acknowledging there was no way this kid was going to make it to the OR. But pushing her instinctive beliefs aside, she made the phone call and then hurried over to help Eric hang more blood, working in tandem on the rapid infuser.

Their patient's blood pressure continued to fall. And then, when the thoracic surgeon walked in, the young man lost his heart rhythm altogether.

"Start CPR," Brock demanded.

Elana jumped up on a stool so she could reach the patient and began doing chest compressions. The image of Brock doing this for Felicity, with a broken collarbone sticking out of his chest, flashed in her mind. Eric took over with the breathing, using the ambu bag to provide deep breaths. She kept up a steady stream of compressions, checking the heart monitor overhead to make sure she was getting good circulation from her efforts.

"He's gone, Brock," the thoracic surgeon said. "I wouldn't take him to surgery in this condition anyway. He's bleeding from everywhere, likely into his head and his abdomen as well as into his chest. There's nothing we can do."

Elana continued to do CPR, after Eric gave epinephrine through the IV, until Brock said, "All right, stop CPR."

She paused, glancing up at the monitor. Flat-line

pulse. Completely absent blood pressure. She let out a heavy sigh.

"Time of death, ten forty-five p.m." Brock's voice was hard, tense, as he stripped off his bloody gloves and grabbed the death notice out of the chart. He scribbled his name on the bottom and then stalked away.

Elana helped Eric clean up the patient, whose family had yet to be notified, but she kept looking for Brock, wondering where he was. She tried to tell herself Brock's issues were none of her business, but she couldn't seem to shut off her concern. When they'd finished cleaning up the patient, waiting for transportation to the morgue, she slipped out of the trauma bay. Following her instincts, she headed towards the staff lounge, catching sight of Brock sitting on the small sofa, his head cradled in his hands.

She felt sick to her stomach, seeing him so miserable. Once she'd wanted him to hurt as much as she did. Now she knew that wasn't true.

Seeing Brock suffer didn't make her feel one bit better.

He was taking the young man's death very hard. Did he always react like this when he lost a patient? She watched him for a minute, realizing he'd probably rather be alone, but, as before, unable to simply walk away.

Had it been just a few short hours since he'd held her when she'd cried outside her mother's nursing home?

"Brock? Are you okay?" she asked, cautiously venturing into the room.

He lifted his head, his expression haggard. "Yeah."

She didn't believe him. He looked awful, and suddenly she understood. He lived for his work, pouring every bit of himself into his patients' lives, taking every death as a personal failure. "Don't do this," she pleaded in a low tone. "It's not your fault. He was gone before he got here."

A flash of anguish flitted across his face before he glanced away. "I know that. I'm not blaming myself."

Yes, he was. The stark desolation on his face proved it. He hated losing even one patient, although every doctor knew that it was impossible to save everyone.

Why did he let it affect him so much? Because of the past? Because of her sister?

She remembered how she'd been at the beginning of her career when she'd lost a patient. "During my first six months in the ED, I lost my first patient. She was in her mid-thirties, but I kept seeing Felicity's face instead of hers."

For a moment his stunned gaze collided with hers. And she realized he was doing the same thing.

She and Brock had more in common than she'd ever imagined.

Chloe had tried to tell her that he'd suffered too, but she'd refused to believe. Hadn't understood how much she'd needed to blame Brock.

Because the only other option was to blame Felicity. For being reckless in pulling out in front of Brock. For being careless in not wearing her seat belt.

For leaving Elana when she'd needed her older sister the most.

The realization shook her to the core. She didn't

want to think about how lost she'd been. At the moment, Brock was more important.

"This isn't the first patient I've lost," he murmured, rubbing a hand over his jaw. "And I'm sure it won't be the last."

Didn't he ever remember the patients he'd saved?

"Jamie Edgar, the spinal fracture patient, is doing fine; she still has some limited mobility, but the spine surgeons have complete confidence she'll regain most of her limb function. Mr Reeves, our heart attack patient, is scheduled to go home tomorrow; he's doing great. Our twin gun-shot victims are also fine, although hospital administration has kept them on opposite ends of the hospital to keep their families from running into each other and causing more fights." She paused, knowing she was forgetting one. "Oh, yes, and Ariel Peterson is doing better too after her drug overdose; her parents have agreed to take her in for therapy."

"So?" Brock had frowned as she'd rattled off just a few of the patients they'd cared for over the past few days. "Saving lives is what we do. What's your point?"

"Focusing on the few losses among so many successes is counterproductive. Stop punishing yourself for losing a patient. Especially one that had so many strikes against him."

He stared at her for a moment, his guilt clearly reflected in his eyes.

"And maybe it's time to stop punishing yourself for Felicity's death."

He glanced away, letting out a harsh laugh. "Strange

advice coming from the woman who hasn't been able to forgive me."

Feeling sucker-punched, she drew in a sharp breath. "Maybe you're right."

He winced and shook his head. "No, don't listen to me. It's been a rough night. I don't know what I'm talking about."

"Yes, you do. Because you're right." She remembered what Eric had said to her less than an hour ago. Pretending everything was fine was hardly healthy. She thought about the hours of pain she'd suffered, the relentless anger as she'd entered the foster-home system. Until Chloe.

Her foster mother had been right all along. She'd thought she'd put the past behind her, but in reality she'd only been pretending. On the surface. Not accepting the truth deep inside where it counted.

Brock Madison wasn't the awful person she'd depicted all these years. Even her mother didn't blame him! Why was she holding back?

"I forgive you."

CHAPTER EIGHT

HE COULDN'T believe what he was hearing. Had she really meant what she'd just said? "It's okay, Elana. You don't have to say things you don't mean to make me feel better. I know I don't deserve your forgiveness."

She let out a heavy sigh. "I'm not putting the past behind me for your sake, Brock. I'm doing it for mine. I think it's time I move forward with my life, don't you?"

"Yes." He was happy for her and seriously hoped she could really follow through. "I'm glad. You deserve to be happy."

Tilting her head to the side, she sent him a puzzled glance. "And you don't?"

He hesitated, unsure how to respond. "Sure, I guess."

He must not have sounded convincing because she gave him a skeptical look. "Have you ever been in a serious relationship?"

"No." He didn't want to have this conversation. He'd rather bask in the knowledge that Elana had forgiven him, even if only for her own sake.

"I see." Her expression was troubled, and he didn't like to think she could read his guilt-ridden mind.

"There hasn't been time," he protested, even though he knew it wasn't really true. "Besides, saving lives is far more important."

"More important than living your own life?" she asked.

Yes. But he didn't say it out loud.

"One isn't mutually exclusive of the other," she said softly.

"I know." Logically he did know, but deep down he couldn't quite accept it. Especially when he thought about those breathtaking moments when their fingers had tangled on the clipboard. Maybe he was thinking about having a personal life for the first time in years, but Elana was off-limits.

Just because she'd forgiven him, didn't mean she wanted to be friends with him. Or more.

Definitely not more.

"I'll see you at work, Brock." She stood and headed towards the door.

He wanted to call her back but forced himself to let her go. He needed to get over his fascination with Elana once and for all. She was a beautiful, successful woman. One he could admire from afar.

He'd find consolation in knowing that now that she'd forgiven him, she wouldn't have to leave the ED and trauma nursing.

His house was dark when he pulled into the driveway, indicating Lacey and Tucker were sleeping.

A flash of guilt plagued him as he walked inside. He

should have called Lacey to find out how Tucker was doing. He was sure the baby would be fine once he had a couple of doses of antibiotics on board, and it wasn't as if he'd had a lot of spare time, since the trauma bay had been jumping, but, still, he should have called.

His brother should be here too, dammit. He'd have to call Rufus Kingsley, the private investigator he'd hired, to see if the guy had made any progress on finding Joel.

Exhausted, he didn't stop by Lacey's room to look in on them. The house was blissfully silent. Carefully, so as not to wake them, he tiptoed past their room, heading for his.

He closed his eyes, hoping the turmoil in his brain would ease with some badly needed sleep.

But, instead, he dreamed about Elana. Only, this time, his subconscious hadn't been satisfied with her gift of forgiveness. He'd wanted more. And when she melted into his arms, she wasn't crying. She was gazing up at him in wonder, wrapping her arms around his neck and kissing him.

He was sweating when Tucker's crying woke him up the next morning at six sharp. Groaning, he turned over and pulled his pillow over his head to drown out the sound. More than anything he wanted to go back to the steamy, erotic Elana of his dreams. Even if she was just a figment of his imagination.

But what if Lacey needed help? What if the baby really wasn't doing any better?

The image of a ready and willing Elana evaporated, and he dragged himself upright and yanked on a pair of sweats.

Blinking the remains of sleep from his eyes, he made his way into the kitchen. Lacey glanced up when he walked in, and he considered it progress when she didn't jump like a scared squirrel.

"Are the antibiotics staying down?" he asked, eyeing the crying baby propped on the table.

"Yesterday the medicine stayed down, but this morning he threw them up," Lacey said, her eyes mirroring his exhaustion. Immediately he felt guilty about wanting to sleep in. Obviously rest and relaxation wasn't an option for Lacey. "I wasn't sure if I should try to get him to take another dose or not."

"I wouldn't," he said, scrubbing a hand over his face. "Did he get up during the night?"

Lacey nodded, her expression still troubled. "I fed him right away so he wouldn't wake you up."

Considerate. Lacey must still feel as if she was imposing. She didn't ask about Joel, though. He wondered if she feared his brother was gone for good.

"Give him some of the rehydration solution," he suggested. "If he's throwing up, he might be a bit dehydrated."

"All right." Lacey pulled herself up from the table to get a bottle of the sugar water. Brock had to admit, if Tucker didn't start feeling better soon, they'd have to take him to the hospital for IV antibiotics.

He needed to get Elana out of his mind. She didn't need him, but Lacey and Tucker did.

And Tucker's health took priority over his useless dreams.

* * *

Brock called Rufus Kingsley, leaving a message for the PI to call him back. Rufus called back within the hour.

"I think I might know where your boy has gone," he said in lieu of a greeting. "Does your uncle have a cabin in the middle of the woods in Marshfield, Wisconsin?"

"Yeah." Why hadn't he considered the possibility of the cabin? His uncle and his father used it for deer hunting, a sport Brock couldn't get into, but Joel used to go up with them every year. "Do you think that's where he is?"

"Possibility, although from what I hear, it's not exactly a nice place to live year-round. April is still pretty cold at night; if he's there, I'm sure he's freezing his butt off. I'm heading there now and will let you know."

Finally, progress on finding his brother. Elana's words came back to him. *You can't force him to be a father.* Muffling the voice in his head, he agreed, "Sounds good. I don't know exactly where it is, but my uncle Joe will probably tell you. His number is in the book."

"Already on it," Rufus said. "I'll keep you posted."

"Thanks." When Brock hung up, he saw Lacey had been listening in. "We might know where Joel is."

"I heard." The expression in her eyes didn't change. Maybe she already knew that finding Joel didn't mean the end to her problems. There was no guarantee he'd be back to help her with Tucker.

Brock turned his attention to Tucker. The baby wasn't eating very well and had stopped taking the sugar water.

After trying without success to get the baby to take any form of nourishment, he gave up. Three hours had passed, and Tucker had only gotten worse instead of better.

"Lacey, we need to take Tucker to the hospital," he said, trying to hide the extent of his concern. "I think he needs IV fluids and IV antibiotics."

"Okay." Her listless response wasn't encouraging. But she rose to her feet and began dressing the baby in his quilted jacket before securing him safely in his infant car seat.

He drove Lacey and Tucker to Children's Memorial Hospital, located opposite the Trinity Medical Center. Because of Tucker's young age, the triage nurse didn't make them wait but hustled them straight back to one of the empty ED rooms. Since Lacey was still looking frazzled, he took the baby into his arms, unzipping his outfit so he wouldn't get too warm.

"What's going on with this little guy?" Dr Barb Wynn asked as she came into the room.

He recognized the doctor from an emergency medicine conference in Las Vegas last year, even though he didn't really know the woman personally. He was happy to see a familiar face. "He has bilateral ear infections but isn't keeping the antibiotics down. I think he's dehydrated and may need IV fluids."

"So why did you come to see me if you have everything all figured out?" Barb teased, taking the baby so she could set him on the edge of the crib to examine him.

"Because you're the pediatric expert, and I'm not," Brock said dryly. "And as long as you're looking at him, his lungs have sounded a bit congested as well; it's possible there's more going on than just a bilateral ear infection."

"Hmm." Barb Wynn listened to Tucker's heart and

lungs. "I agree; I don't like the way he sounds," she admitted. "His ear infections may have already progressed to something more serious, like bronchitis or pneumonia. We'll get a chest X-ray and some blood cultures. I'll have one of the nurses come in to start an IV."

Lacey made a small sound of protest but didn't voice her concern. Brock belatedly introduced them. "Lacey is Tucker's mom; my brother, Joel, is the father. Joel's not available at the moment."

"Nice to meet you, Lacey. Don't worry, we'll take good care of Tucker, I promise."

Lacey's attempt at a smile was truly pathetic. As Barb Wynn left to get her orders written, he tried to put her at ease, suspecting she was blaming herself for not being a good mother.

"This isn't your fault, Lacey. Kids get sick all the time. Once Tucker gets a few doses of IV antibiotics, he'll be much better, you'll see."

"I'm sure you're right," Lacey said in a quiet voice.

"Of course I'm right." Brock glanced at his vibrating phone. "I'll be right back, all right?"

Without waiting for her to respond, he opened his phone and walked out towards the waiting room so his cell phone wouldn't interfere with any of the monitoring equipment.

"Hello?"

"Brock? Rufus here. I'm at your uncle's cabin. The good news is that Joel has been here: the fire in the fireplace is fresh, and there are muddy footprints outside. The bad news is that he's gone."

Gone? How was that possible? He glanced back through the doorway leading into the emergency department and the small room where he'd left Tucker and Lacey. Even now, he could hear the baby crying, no doubt as he was getting poked with the IV.

Joel should be here, supporting Lacey. And Tucker.

Where on earth could his brother be?

Elana went into work early on Monday, a few hours before the start of her shift. She'd decided to come in early to complete some education modules that she hadn't quite finished, since sitting around at home and thinking about Brock was driving her crazy.

She'd meant what she'd said about forgiving him for her own sake rather than his. But saying the words, and believing them deep down where it counted, was much more difficult. She'd wanted to find Chloe, since talking to her foster mother had always helped in the past, but Chloe, well on the road to recovery from her operation, was helping to set up a charity function at the local church. And Elana was scheduled to work.

Raine was in the arena, her eyes widening in surprise when she saw Elana. "What are you doing here? Did you get called in early too?"

"No, just thought I'd finish that disaster planning module that's due the end of the quarter," Elana said. She glanced around, hoping she wasn't being too obvious. "Have you seen Brock?"

"Ah, yeah, in fact I have." Raine's expression was pained, and she grabbed Elana's arm, tugging her into the break room. "Look, Elana, I don't know how to tell you this."

Perplexed, she arched a brow. "Tell me what?"

"Brock's here. In the cafeteria." Raine's eyes were grim. "I just saw him down there while I was getting lunch, and you need to know, he's not alone. He's sitting with—a woman."

Elana's heart stumbled in her chest. Brock was with another woman? She swallowed hard, feeling sick. She'd gotten the impression he wasn't seeing anyone. That he'd given up on having a personal life at all. The stab of jealousy struck deep.

"She's not at all the sort of woman I'd expect him to be with," Raine continued. "She's too young, rail thin, with stringy blonde hair. Pretty enough, I guess, if a guy is into the lost-waif type."

Lacey. Irrational relief flooded her. Raine's description fit Lacey to a T. "Was there a baby with them?"

Raine's eyes rounded comically. "Oh, my God, you mean to tell me Dr Madison has a kid?" she squeaked.

"No, the baby is his brother's child," Elana explained quickly. "And I think the woman he's with is Lacey, his brother's girlfriend. Don't you remember? They were at the clinic this past Saturday."

Raine didn't look entirely convinced. "No, I don't remember. For your sake I hope you're right."

"Brock's personal life isn't any of my business," she said, even though she knew she wasn't being truthful. Because she did care if there was a special woman in Brock's life. More than she should.

"Yeah, right." Raine rolled her eyes.

Elana ignored her. "I think I'll run down to check on them. It's odd they're here in the cafeteria." She tried to sound nonchalant so Raine wouldn't guess at how invested she was in Lacey's situation. The poor girl had already been through so much.

A horrible thought hit hard. What if they'd found Joel? And he was right now a patient up in the ICU?

"Don't say I didn't warn you," Raine said.

Elana gave a distracted nod, turned and left. Thankfully she hadn't swiped in yet to officially start work.

Bypassing the pokey elevator in favor of the stairs, she ran down to the cafeteria, not even realizing she was holding her breath as she scanned the crowd, looking for Brock. When she saw him sitting in a booth along the back wall, facing Lacey, she let out her pent-up breath in a rush.

She'd been right. He wasn't with another woman. She frowned when she realized Tucker's infant seat wasn't anywhere in sight.

They were arguing, or, to be technically correct, Brock was arguing while Lacey just sat with her thin shoulders hunched defensively.

"Why are you being so stubborn?" he asked, clearly annoyed as he pushed a set of car keys across the table towards Lacey. "This is your chance to take a break, to do something for yourself. You know Tucker's in good hands."

Lacey's eyes were downcast, as if she could barely hold Brock's gaze. "I don't need a break. I told you, I'm fine."

"You're fine." Brock let out a rough laugh. In an abrupt move, he reached across the table and grabbed her arm, roughly pushing up her sleeve to expose the cut oozing on her forearm. "Sure, you're fine. If you're so fine, why are you cutting yourself, huh?"

Lacey twisted her arm from his grip, shrinking further back against the seat. Elana sucked in a harsh breath at the flash of pure panic in Lacey's eyes. She hurried forward.

"Hi, Lacey, Brock. What are you guys doing here?" She smiled brightly, ignoring the tension as she glanced around. "Where's Tucker?"

There was a long moment of silence before Brock turned to her. "Tucker has pneumonia; he's been admitted to Children's Memorial."

"Oh, no, I'm sorry. I didn't know." Truly distressed by the news, she glanced at Lacey, who looked much worse than Raine had described her. The poor thing looked as if she hadn't gotten any sleep in days. "Is he doing all right?"

Brock nodded, again answering for Lacey. "He was admitted yesterday and he's on IV antibiotics. They're pleased with his progress so far."

Lacey's hand shot out, her fingers curling around the keys Brock had shoved in her direction. "I think I will borrow your car; I do have a few errands to run."

Brock looked surprised at Lacey's change of heart. "Good. I'm glad."

"Excuse me," Lacey whispered, easing out of the booth. She clutched her ragged purse beneath her arm and left.

Elana watched her for a moment before turning to Brock. "You scared her to death," she accused as she slid into Lacey's vacated spot.

"I didn't mean to." Brock looked truly bewildered.

"It's your anger that scares her," Elana explained. "She thinks you don't like her."

Brock scrubbed his face with his hands. He didn't look as if he'd gotten much sleep, either. "Of course I like her. She's the mother of my nephew. I'm trying to support her as best I can."

"Lacey needs to know you don't resent her. And that you'll be there for the long haul."

Brock grimaced. "You're probably right. The private investigator I hired found where Joel had been staying at a remote cabin in the north woods that my uncle owns, but Joel's not there now. I'm sure that information isn't making Lacey feel any better."

"You're right, and yet you chose this moment to confront her about the cuts on her arm."

"Am I supposed to ignore what she's doing to herself?" he asked. "Why do you think I was so insistent that she take the keys?"

She let out a heavy sigh. Brock's intentions had been good, but his technique needed work. "I don't know what to tell you. Lacey needs help. Maybe there are some counseling services for low-income families. I'll ask around, see what's available."

"Thank you," Brock said quietly. "I appreciate your help."

There was an awkward moment of silence. She knew

she should go back up to the ED to work on her modules, but she didn't move. She hadn't seen Brock alone since the night they'd worked together and he'd lost his young patient.

Since she'd told him she'd forgiven him.

Since she'd realized he'd planned to sacrifice his own life in order to save others.

"Elana, did you mean what you said?" Brock's intense gaze bored into hers. The noisy, crowded cafeteria faded away, making her feel as if they were the only two people in the room. "About trying to find a way to forgive me?"

"Yes." She flashed a crooked smile. "Sometimes it's easy to forget when we're sitting here like this, talking about Lacey and Tucker. But other times—" she gave a helpless shrug "—it's not as easy to forget. And then I find myself thinking the worst."

Brock nodded, his expression serious. "I understand. And I want you to know how much it means to me that you're willing to try. You were right, though, to do it for you, not for me."

She almost shook her head because he was wrong. Brock needed her forgiveness as much as she needed to give it. What a messed-up pair they were.

She bit back a protest when he stood. "I have to get back to Tucker," he said in a low voice.

Stifling her regret, Elana stood too. "Are you working tonight?"

"Yeah, although you'll probably be glad to hear I'm working a shorter shift; I'm splitting the time with

Nathan Forrester." His lopsided smile did funny things to her stomach.

When he turned to walk away, Elana realized, with a start, that he was wrong. Again.

She wasn't glad to hear he was working a short shift. As irrational as it was, she looked forward to working with Brock.

She missed him when he wasn't there.

CHAPTER NINE

ELANA was assigned to the trauma room with Brock. From the beginning of their shift, it was busy. Their first two patients were elderly women with severe flu symptoms.

It took a while to get the patients admitted to the ICU, where they belonged, because every critical care bed was full. Finally, after almost two hours, Elana was able to transfer both patients upstairs.

By the time she'd returned, the trauma pager was going off again. Brock met her in the trauma bay, a slight frown marring his forehead.

"Motor vehicle crash," he said in a low tone.

She nodded, having read the text message herself.

Female driver, Janey Thompson, in critical condition after long extrication.

"Get ready," Brock murmured.

She took a deep breath just as the doors of the trauma bay burst open. Two paramedics wheeled their patient in, and, as Janey Thompson drew closer, Elana looked down, and her heart lodged in her throat.

Janey Thompson was young. Far younger than she'd expected. Beneath the blood stains and open gash on her forehead, Janey couldn't have been much more than sixteen.

"Dear God," Brock said in a low, shocked tone. She knew he was remembering her sister, Felicity. "Give me the latest set of vitals."

The paramedics rattled them off. "BP low at 66/32. Heart rate extremely tachy at 155 beats per minute. She was intubated in the field, and we've had fluids wide open during the ride over here."

Elana swallowed hard. This young girl already had so many strikes against her. She feared their efforts would be in vain.

"Get two units of O-negative blood in her stat, Elana," Brock ordered, his expression grim. "We are not going to lose her."

She believed him. With renewed energy, she reached for the two units of packed red blood cells and hung them on the rapid infuser. Since Eric Towne was preoccupied with another patient from the same crash, she and Brock worked over young Janey together.

As the blood was flowing in, she performed a quick assessment. "Brock, take a look. The right side of her chest is tense and hard; I think she has a tension pneumothorax."

At that moment, the monitor overhead began alarming. They'd lost her blood pressure!

"Get me an eighteen gauge needle," he ordered, ripping off the girl's blouse to expose her ribs.

Elana whipped open the top drawer of the supply cabinet and grabbed the needle. Without taking the time to prep the skin, Brock yanked on gloves and stabbed the needle between the patient's fourth and fifth ribs.

"It's working," Elana said urgently, her eyes glued to the monitor. "Her blood pressure is coming back up."

"We need a chest tube set up." Brock's expression was still tense. "I think she's bleeding into her chest. And I want a CT surgery consult."

She was already pulling out the chest tube insertion tray. Brock had taken care of the immediate crisis with the tension pneumothorax, but Janey wasn't out of the woods yet.

Brock inserted the chest tube, and immediately the tubing filled with blood. Elana called the operator to order a stat surgery consult.

Between them, they worked in tandem over Janey Thompson, giving fluids and blood, for well over an hour. Sweat was dripping down her spine when they finally had Janey stabilized enough for surgery.

"Let's get her up to the OR," Brock said.

With a nod, she disconnected the young girl from the monitor above the bed and connected her to the portable device they used for transports. She wasn't at all surprised when Brock helped her to wheel Janey upstairs.

The surgical team met them right outside the OR doors. With one last look at Janey's pale face, Elana stepped back and let the OR team take over.

For a long moment, Brock didn't move.

"You did it," Elana whispered, touching his hand lightly. "You saved her."

Brock slowly shook his head, a relieved half smile curving his mouth. "Not just me. You too. We saved her, Elana. Together."

"Together," she echoed. Janey had a fighting chance to make it, thanks to her and Brock's teamwork. Maybe it could always be this way between them? Maybe this was meant to be?

In companionable silence, they headed back down to the trauma room.

Dr Nathan Forrester was already there, waiting for them. "Hey, Brock, I was able to get here a little early, so you're free to get out of here."

She struggled to hide her dismay. She'd forgotten about Brock's plans to work a short shift.

"I appreciate it, Nate." Brock glanced at Elana, his blue gaze intense, and for a brief moment, he made her feel as if they were all alone in the room. "Thanks again for all your help, Elana."

"You're welcome." She licked suddenly dry lips, wishing he didn't have to go. She tried to remember they were both simply doing their jobs, but it seemed like so much more.

Because together they'd made an awesome team.

The rest of Elana's shift dragged by. Not that Dr Forrester wasn't a good doctor, because he was. But, somehow, working the trauma bay with him wasn't nearly as exciting as working with Brock. His intensity drew out the best in the rest of them.

"Elana?" The unit clerk called out to her as she was about to head to the locker room. "You have a call on line two."

She frowned, wondering who would call her this late. Chloe? She quickened her step and picked up the closest phone. "Hello?"

"Elana? It's Brock. I need your help."

Her fingers tightened on the phone. "Tucker? Is he okay?"

"Tucker's fine, but Lacey's gone. She's not answering her phone, and I haven't seen her since I gave her my car keys at lunchtime."

"Gone?" Elana frowned. Surely Brock was exaggerating. "Are you sure?"

"I need a ride," Brock said bluntly. "I'm still at Children's. Are you able to drive me home when you're finished with work?"

"Of course. I'm finished now. Give me five minutes, and I'll pick you up outside."

Elana hung up the phone, her mind whirling. There had to be some sort of explanation. Lacey wouldn't just take off, leaving Tucker behind, especially in Brock's car. Lacey was intimidated by Brock.

There must be some mistake. More likely, Lacey had gone back to Brock's house and had fallen sound asleep. The poor thing probably hadn't had a decent night's sleep since before Tucker was born.

She hurried to the parking garage. Minutes later, she

pulled up at the front door of Children's Memorial Hospital. Brock strode out, and he would have been devastatingly handsome in his worn blue jeans and navy-blue shirt if not for the dark frown etched on his features.

"I appreciate the lift," he said brusquely.

"No problem." His broad shoulders bumped into hers as he leaned back and over to put his seat belt on. She grabbed the steering wheel tightly, hyperaware of his overwhelming presence in her small car. Everything felt different now that she'd forgiven him. Especially after the closeness they'd shared working over Janey. "How long do you think they're going to keep Tucker in the hospital?"

"The plan at this point is to keep him for three days on IV antibiotics before switching him to oral medication. If he does well, he could potentially come home as early as Wednesday."

"That's good to know." Elana glanced at him. "You tried calling Lacey at home?"

"At least a dozen times." His expression turned even darker, and Elana knew he was thinking the worst.

She didn't argue because nothing she could say would make him feel any better. Ten minutes later, when she pulled into his driveway, she saw the garage door was closed and there were no lights on anywhere inside the house.

It certainly looked as if no one was home.

Brock jumped out of the car before she'd even put it in park, using his key to access the house. She quickly followed him inside, suddenly feeling extremely apprehensive. Their young patient, Ariel Peterson, had taken an overdose of drugs. What if Lacey had done something similar?

"Lacey? Are you here?" Brock shouted as he strode through the house, flipping on light switches wherever he went. He headed straight into Lacey's room but came back out so fast Elana knew he hadn't found her.

Brock headed through the living room into the kitchen and through to the garage, probably checking the garage for his car. With her pulse pounding, Elana forced herself to check the bathroom, pushing back the shower curtain to look inside the bathtub, making sure Lacey wasn't lying there. Then she even went so far as to check Brock's room but didn't find any evidence that Lacey had been there, either.

"She took off and left her son," Brock said grimly when they met back in the living room. "I just checked her bedroom again. Some of her stuff is gone, along with the small suitcase she had, but Tucker's things are all here."

"I can't believe it," she murmured. This truly didn't look good, and she would have easily bet money that Lacey would never willingly abandon her child. "Maybe she just lost track of time. I'm sure she'll be back."

His bark of laughter held no humor. "Yeah, that's what I told her when Joel took off, and you can see how well that worked out for me. At least Joel didn't steal my car."

"You gave her the keys," Elana pointed out. "That's not stealing. Besides, even the police wouldn't do anything anyway, not until she's been gone twenty-four hours. We haven't seen her since noon, and it's close to midnight now. I'm sure she'll show up sometime tomor-row." At least, she hoped so.

Brock rubbed a hand along the back of his neck. "I really screwed everything up, didn't I?"

"No." When he grimaced, obviously not believing her, she shrugged. "Maybe. But Lacey is tougher than you think."

His shoulders slumped, and he sank down on the sofa, looking like a man defeated. "You were right, earlier. I shouldn't have confronted her about the cuts on her arm. I don't know what I was thinking."

Hearing the self-recrimination in his tone, she sat down beside him. "Hey, don't be too hard on yourself. You moved here just to support your brother and Lacey. That counts for something."

He slowly shook his head. "I lost my temper and snapped at her. No wonder she took off."

"Do you know anything about her background?" she asked, changing the subject. "Does Lacey have family in the area?"

"I have no idea. She's been pretty quiet about her past. But I do care about her," he said, lifting his head to meet her gaze. "I care about Lacey and Tucker. And I care about Joel too, even though I've been irritated with him since he left."

"Understandable, don't you think?" she asked softly, taking his hand in hers and giving it a reassur-ing squeeze.

He lifted their clasped hands and brushed a kiss across her knuckles, the soft caress sending tingles down her spine. She couldn't have moved away from him now if her life depended on it.

"The minute I realized Lacey was gone, I wanted to call you. This is the second time you've come to my rescue, Elana."

Her mouth went dry, but she tried to smile. "Like I said before, I don't mind."

Brock closed his eyes and sat back against the sofa. She sat back too, intending to stay only for a few more minutes. He put his arm around her shoulders and hugged her close. The gesture was nice. Comforting. She should leave to go home, but she didn't want to. She liked being here with Brock.

Secretly savoring the embrace, her eyes drifted closed, and she wished for the impossible.

When Brock opened his eyes several hours later to see the bright sunlight streaming in through the windows, he realized they'd fallen asleep on his sofa. Elana's soft body was pressed against him, the curves of her body achingly noticeable through her thin scrubs. Somehow, during the night, they must have stretched out on the sofa, instinctively seeking a more comfortable position.

Her warm vanilla scent teased his senses. Brock knew he should move, especially now that every nerve in his body had zinged to awareness, his groin tightening with primitive need, making his jeans uncomfortably snug. Holding Elana in his arms felt good. Better than good. Fantastic.

He wanted her. More than he'd ever wanted any other

woman in a really long time. He'd been determined to stay away from her, but he was fighting a losing battle. Because he didn't want to stay away. He liked working with her. The way they'd saved Janey had given him hope. Had made him realize how great it was working with Elana.

Or maybe it was enough to simply be with Elana.

Breathing in her scent, he didn't move, unwilling to do anything that might bring this slice of heaven to an end. When Elana shifted, pressing her body against his, he held his breath. Her hand splayed in the center of his chest, the heat of her palm burning through the thin fabric of his shirt. He froze, hoping and praying she wouldn't wake up.

Not yet.

Her hand lightly caressed him, her fingertips making lazy circles that sent a shaft of desire straight to his groin. Holding her like this was pure, agonizing torture.

But he didn't want to be anywhere else.

Elana shifted again, her lips skimming the line of his jaw, and in that moment, it occurred to him that she might be awake.

Was it possible?

After everything that had happened in the past twenty-four hours, was it possible she was really awake? Wanting him as much as he wanted her?

Afraid to breathe, he trailed his hand up along her arm, wishing the thin, long-sleeved T-shirt she wore beneath her scrubs would vanish, so he could relish the silky softness of her skin. His fingers brushed along the side of her breast, and she reflexively arched against him, as if seeking more.

He lifted his head to glance down at her, to make sure she wasn't still asleep and unaware of what was happening. When she gazed up at him, he knew she was silently encouraging him to continue. He lowered his head and captured her mouth in a dizzying kiss.

Her fingers curled in the fabric of his shirt, not to push him away, but to hold on to him, as she, hesitantly at first, and then with more boldness, kissed him back.

CHAPTER TEN

BROCK's heart soared. Drowning in the taste of her, he slanted his mouth over hers, deepening the kiss. He wanted Elana more than he wanted to breathe.

He could have stayed like this forever. But the heat of her skin beckoned.

Slowly, he slid a hand beneath her scrubs, seeking the softness beneath. She stiffened and drew back, gasping for breath. "Wait."

Wait? He forced himself to stop, to pull back, even though every nerve in his body wanted more. He lifted his head and gulped desperately needed oxygen into his lungs. "What's wrong?"

"Nothing. Everything." Elana pushed against his chest again, and this time he reluctantly released her. She smoothed a hand through her hair. "I—we can't do this."

He tried to gather his scattered thoughts. Had he imagined her response? He didn't think so.

"I can't believe I fell asleep," she continued. "Gosh, it's later than I thought. I really need to get home."

He didn't know what he'd done to cause her to back

away, but there was no denying that, despite her sweet response, she now regretted their kiss.

The way she avoided his gaze bothered him. He put a hand on her arm to keep her from bolting for the door. "Do I need to apologize, Elana? If so, I'm sorry. I never meant to make you feel uncomfortable."

She tugged from his grasp and leaped to her feet, straightening her clothes. "You didn't make me uncomfortable," she said, although the rush of color in her cheeks belied her words. "I just don't want you to think I stayed—for this."

"We fell asleep. It's not a crime." He stared at her for a moment, quickly figuring out that she hadn't been awake as long as he'd thought. She'd enjoyed their kiss, but he'd let things get a little too far out of control.

His fault, not hers. But after that kiss, he didn't want her to leave. "I'm sorry," he said again. "Would you please stay for breakfast?" Brock slowly rose to his feet. "You'd actually be doing me a favor since I'm going to need a ride back to Children's Memorial anyway."

"Oh." She hesitated, looking like a scared fawn ready to bolt. "I—uh, sure. I guess I can take you back to the hospital; it's on my way."

"So you'll let me make you breakfast?" he asked hopefully, wishing he could do something to help her relax. No matter what she said, he had obviously made her uncomfortable, and for that he was sorry. "The bathroom is right down the hall, and you can help yourself to whatever you need; there's a new toothbrush in the cabinet."

"All right, you can make me breakfast," she acquiesced. "And I will borrow your bathroom if you don't mind."

"Take all the time you need." When she disappeared into the bathroom, he scrubbed his hands over his face, grateful for the time to pull himself together.

That kiss had shaken him. Had tied his stomach into knots and left him wanting more.

But Elana wasn't at ease with him, and, really, could he blame her? She'd barely had time to come to grips with forgiving him, much less understand why he'd kissed her senseless.

He needed to take things slowly. To give her time to get used to him. As a friend and, maybe in time, as something more.

He didn't feel the same sense of panic he usually did when faced with an attractive woman he'd wanted to get to know better. He usually avoided relationships. But for the first time in his life, he couldn't make himself back away, even though he knew he didn't deserve her.

Keeping busy in the kitchen, making omelets for breakfast, helped him stay focused, but when Elana returned, with her face scrubbed free of makeup and her hair brushed, gently framing her face, darned if he didn't feel another shaft of desire.

She was so beautiful, his gut ached.

"Coffee?" he asked in a low, husky tone.

"Yes, please."

He pulled another mug out of the cupboard, taking several deep breaths to steady his hands as he poured her a cup. He knew she preferred flavored creamer, but he didn't have any. "I'm sorry, but I only have milk," he said, pushing the container towards her.

"That's fine." Again, she avoided his direct gaze, and he wondered what she was thinking. Did she regret the heated kiss they'd shared?

"Are you planning to call the police about Lacey taking your car?" she asked as he slid twin ham-and-cheese omelets on two plates, one for each of them, and set them on the table.

"No. But I might call Rufus, the private investigator," he said. "I do need to get my car back eventually. But I'd rather give Lacey a chance to return the vehicle on her own. And I'm truly more worried about what might happen to Tucker than about the stupid car."

"I'm glad," Elana murmured. She stared at him for a long moment before she turned her attention to her food. Softly she added, "You're a nice man, Brock."

The bite of omelet lodged in the back of his throat.

No, he wasn't a nice man. Because if she knew what erotic thoughts had been going through his mind all morning, Elana would surely turn and run as fast as she could in the opposite direction.

And he wouldn't blame her one bit.

Elana tried to eat her omelet, anxious to act as if everything was normal, but, in reality, the effects of Brock's kiss had left her badly shaken.

Brock may have started the kiss, but she'd been more than a willing participant. Until the moment he'd slid his hand beneath her scrubs, reminding her how long it had been since she'd been naked and vulnerable with a man.

Too long.

Forever.

She shied away from that thought.

"This is great," she said, forcing enthusiasm into her tone, even though for all she could tell, she might be eating sawdust. She swallowed hard, anxious to finish so she could get out of Brock's house. Away from the sofa that mocked her.

Her cell phone rang, drawing her gaze back to her purse that was still on the sofa. Odd, she wasn't expecting a call. "Excuse me," she murmured.

She went into the living room and fished her phone out from the depths of her purse. The number on the screen indicated the call was from the hospital. Her boss asking her to come in early? She hesitated, tempted to let it go to voice mail.

"Hello?"

"Elana? This is Claire, the manager of the ICU. I received your transfer request from Human Resources. Would you have time this afternoon to stop in for an interview?"

She flashed a guilty glance at Brock, who was watching her. This was the call she'd been waiting for, only now she wasn't sure she still was interested in transferring out of the ED. Away from Brock. Working with Brock as they'd taken care of Janey had been extremely rewarding.

She didn't want to leave him.

But she wasn't going to make a hasty decision. It certainly wouldn't hurt to find out more about the position before making a final decision. "Ah, sure. I can do that."

"How about two o'clock?" Claire asked.

"That will be fine." She turned to reach for a pen and paper from her purse.

"Great. My office is on the fourth floor, right across from the ICU. You can't miss it."

She hastily scribbled two o'clock and fourth floor on a scrap piece of paper. "Thanks, I'll see you then." She flipped her phone shut and tossed it back in her purse.

"Problems?" Brock asked when she came back to the kitchen table.

"No, just work." She swallowed her cold omelet, feeling guilty for not telling Brock the truth. But it seemed foolish to bring up the possibility of her transfer when she wasn't even sure she was going to take it. "I have to go in for a meeting."

"I see." She was grateful he let the subject drop.

She finished her food and pushed away her empty plate. "Thanks for breakfast, Brock. You're a great cook."

"You're welcome." As if sensing how desperately she wanted to leave, he stood and carried their empty dishes to the sink. "Would you give me a few minutes to shower and change before we leave?"

"Of course." She smiled weakly, thankful when he'd finally left her alone. For a moment she buried her face in her hands, stifling a low groan.

What had she been thinking, kissing Brock like that?

She'd wantonly pressed against him. Had very nearly thrown caution to the wind and begged for more.

Maybe she should consider that transfer. Because now that she'd kissed Brock, she was acutely aware of him. As a man she was attracted to.

She'd opened herself up to a personal relationship during her college years, but that leap of faith had blown up in her face. She'd never trusted anyone like that again.

Yet here she was, considering placing her trust in Brock. The one man who had the power to hurt her worse than she'd ever been hurt before.

Because she cared about him. Too much for her own good.

Elana drove Brock to Children's Memorial, struggling to maintain the light friendly tone.

"Do you want to come up with me to see Tucker?" Brock asked as she pulled up in front of the hospital.

"Not right now, maybe later," she hedged.

"If you have time, come over after your meeting," he suggested. "I'll be hanging out here for most of the day; I want to talk to the pediatrician when he makes rounds."

"You're not working tonight?" Elana asked.

He shook his head. "Are you?"

"No, I'm off too." Amazing how their schedules seemed to match perfectly. She flashed him a smile. "Take care, Brock. I'll probably see you later."

"Thanks for the ride." He took her hand, gave it a squeeze, and then reluctantly let go and climbed from the car.

"Goodbye." She waved as she pulled away.

Elana headed home, her thoughts in turmoil as she stepped into the shower. The hot spray didn't wash away her sudden doubts.

Was she crazy to even think about staying in the emergency department with Brock?

Maybe. She needed to talk to Raine. Or Chloe. Her foster mother had always been there for Elana when she needed someone to talk to. If anyone could make sense of the confused madness that defined her feelings for Brock, Chloe could.

She threw on a sweater and jeans, allowing her hair to air-dry as she hurried back outside.

"Elana! How nice of you to stop by." Chloe greeted her warmly.

"Oh, Chloe." Elana closed her eyes and savored her foster mother's exuberant embrace, returning the tight hug, inhaling the familiar, comforting scent of roses. Over these past few years, Chloe had become synonymous with home. Elana loved and cared about her mother, but it was Chloe's gentle, no-nonsense attitude that had kept her grounded when times were tough.

Feeling better already, Elana grinned and stepped back from the hug. "How are you feeling?"

"I'm fine." Chloe waved off Elana's concern and gestured for her to come into the living room. They sat down on the sofa, which was soft and threadbare from years of use. Elana turned to face her foster mother, seeking any hint of fatigue or lingering pain. "Completely back to normal."

Reassured that Chloe at least looked well rested, she raised a skeptical brow. "I hope you're following that low-fat diet Dr Ames recommended."

"Of course." Chloe answered so quickly, Elana suspected she was fudging the truth. Chloe loved fried foods and had agreed to try to cut back after her cardiac stent placement. "But enough about my medical issues; I'd rather talk about you. How are you doing? What's new at work?"

She didn't bother sidestepping the issue. "Chloe, you're not going to believe this, but I have two big things to tell you. First of all, my mom started to speak. And secondly, Brock Madison is the new emergency medicine doctor on staff."

Chloe's eyes grew wide. "Oh, my. How wonderful for you about your mother. But Brock Madison? Heavens, how are you holding up?"

"It's been difficult." Elana lifted a shoulder in a slight shrug. "At first, it was impossible. I put in for a transfer to critical care. But the more I work with him, the more I realize he's changed. I don't hate him, Chloe," she said in a rush. "I've wasted so many years, hating him. Even my mother told me not to hate him."

"There, now." Chloe took her hand and squeezed it tight. "You were young. And so full of pain."

Tears pricked her eyelids, and she blinked them back. "I needed someone to blame, and Brock was the perfect target."

"And now?" Chloe asked softly.

"I don't blame him." She drew a deep breath, anxious

to tell Chloe everything. "I can't blame him because I've seen firsthand how he's suffered too. He doesn't deal well with losing patients. And he treats every new patient like a challenge he's not going to lose."

"So he's a good doctor."

"Yes. He's a good doctor. And a good man. He's dedicated his entire life to saving others." She swallowed hard, determined to tell Chloe everything. "I like him. Too much."

Chloe's eyes widened at the implication. "You're attracted to him." It wasn't a question.

"Yes." She couldn't deny it. "I kissed him. But I have an interview this afternoon with the manager of the ICU." Elana jammed her fingers through her damp hair. "Chloe, help me. What should I do?"

"I can't answer that, Elana. Only you can."

Typical—even when she was young, Chloe had made her face her feelings. "I don't know," she whispered helplessly. "I like working with Brock. I think we make a good team."

"So what's stopping you?"

"Fear." Saying it out loud didn't sound as ridiculous as she'd thought. "I'm afraid. Of caring too much. I kissed him, Chloe. And that kiss could have led to something more. Maybe I should transfer to critical care."

"So you're starting this relationship already believing Brock will hurt you?"

"Yes. No." She shook her head. "I don't know."

"There are no guarantees in any relationship, Elana.

I don't think you should leave because you're thinking the worst."

Chloe was right: she was already planning for a contingency in case things didn't work out. "Maybe you're right," she agreed.

"Of course I'm right."

Chloe's certainty made her chuckle. "I guess it's just not easy for me to trust him."

"It could be that he feels the same way. Aren't you afraid you'll be the one to hurt him?" Chloe asked.

"No." The idea had never entered her mind. "He has nurses tripping over themselves to get his attention. He could have anyone he wanted." And she couldn't imagine he really wanted her. Especially since he didn't know the truth about her past.

"Then why did he kiss you?" Chloe asked reasonably. "Don't sell yourself short, Elana. Maybe Brock Madison has kept an eye on you throughout the years."

"No. He was just as surprised to see me working in the ED as I was to see him." The expression on his face when he'd recognized her had been priceless. If she'd been in the right frame of mind to appreciate it. "I'm sure he moved away in the first place because it would be easier to forget."

Chloe pursed her lips for a moment. "Do you really think so?"

She shrugged, remembering how he'd looked when they'd lost the young pedestrian hit by the car. "Maybe not. He's intense. I doubt he ever forgot."

"Elana, I think it's time you knew the truth."

"About what?"

"Your college scholarship." Chloe grimaced. "Brock Madison didn't want you to know, but he sponsored your scholarship."

"What?" She couldn't wrap her mind around the news. "How?"

"He supplied the money," Chloe said simply. "I'm not sure how he did it, although I suspect he doubled the amount of his own student loans to come up with the necessary amount. But, in the end, he went through the university to ensure his scholarship was awarded to you."

"But that's impossible." Dumbfounded, Elana stared at her foster mother.

"He didn't want you to know. And I've honored his request, until now."

"I don't know what to say," Elana murmured, still in shock. Brock had sponsored her scholarship. Likely out of guilt. For years she'd hated him, had blamed him for everything that had gone wrong in her life. Ironic to realize that, without his help, she wouldn't be where she was today. "I never suspected."

"I tried telling you he wasn't a bad person," Chloe reminded her. "But I'm glad you've found a way to forgive him on your own."

She nodded. She had forgiven him, and suddenly that was the easy part. How was she supposed to handle talking to him now that she knew the truth? Humbled, she looked up at Chloe. "I feel like I should pay him back."

Chloe quizzically tilted her head to the side. "Why don't you try trusting him instead?"

Trusting him. With her body and maybe with her heart. She thought about their heated kiss. Maybe Brock could heal her once and for all. "Okay, I'll trust him."

"Follow your heart, Elana." Chloe smiled at her with approval. "Always follow your heart."

"I will, Chloe." She gave her foster mother a warm hug.

Elana dressed in a navy-blue suit, one of the few outfits she owned that was appropriate for a job interview. She'd talk to Claire, but, in reality, she'd already made her decision.

She was going to stay in the ED with Brock.

Claire was nice enough, and when the only position she had was the graveyard shift, it was even easier to decline. As Claire walked her down to the lobby, she asked Elana to keep in touch if anything changed.

"I will. Thanks, Claire."

Brock walked into the lobby, looking surprised to see her standing there with Claire. He narrowed his gaze when he took in her formal attire, immediately realizing she hadn't been truthful about her meeting. She winced, unable to hide the flash of guilt.

"Elana?" He immediately strode towards her. "Wait. Don't make any rash decisions. Let's talk about this first, okay?"

"Brock, this isn't what you think…" she tried to reassure him.

"You're making a mistake," he interrupted, not letting her finish. "Have dinner with me, please? Things have been intense since Lacey vanished, and I could use a break. I borrowed a friend's car. I can pick you up at six. Please, give me a chance."

How could she not? And he was right: things had been intense with Lacey gone. Remembering her promise to Chloe and to her own mother, Elana nodded. "All right, Brock. I'll have dinner with you tonight."

CHAPTER ELEVEN

BROCK finished up with Tucker and then drove Nathan's car home, clenching the steering wheel tightly. He couldn't believe Elana had gone to a job interview. Despite her claims that she'd forgiven him, she was still planning to leave trauma nursing.

Ha. Not if he had anything to say about it.

When he arrived at home, he wasn't too surprised to find that Lacey still hadn't returned.

Maybe he ought to call the police after all. Something could have happened to Lacey. She could be a patient in a hospital somewhere...or worse.

Pushing his troubled thoughts aside, Brock showered again and shaved before changing into slacks and a dress shirt. Elana deserved to go someplace special.

Fancy, yet intimate.

Feeling uncharacteristically nervous, he drove to her house. She met him at her apartment door, wearing a long-sleeved siren-red dress that clung to her generous curves and flared at the knee. He stared at her, his mouth martini dry as he struggled to keep a rein on his desire.

This was his chance to convince her to change her mind, not give her another reason to leave.

"You look stunning," he murmured.

She flashed a shy smile. "Thank you. It was fun dressing up for a change."

She hovered in the doorway, as if afraid to ask him in, so he escorted her back out to the car, wishing there was some way to put her at ease.

"You know, you didn't have to do this," Elana said as he headed toward the restaurant. "I didn't accept the transfer."

"You didn't?" He threw her a startled glance. "Really?"

"Really. I thought about it but decided that I'd rather stay right where I am. For now."

He took a deep breath, relaxing a bit at the news. "I'm glad, Elana. You had me worried for a minute."

"I know. I should have told you the truth about the job interview."

"What made you change your mind?" he asked, curious.

There was a moment of silence before she turned towards him. "You."

Him? His breath lodged in his throat. "I'm glad. This morning I was worried that I'd scared you off."

"Maybe a little at first." She surprised him by acknowledging the truth. "I don't have a lot of experience with relationships."

He almost wanted to laugh, since his experience with relationships was nonexistent too. For years he'd carried so much guilt; he hadn't believed he deserved happiness. A future. But somehow those old arguments didn't seem to matter at the moment. He reached over and took her hand. "Me either. So I guess we'll learn, together."

Her smile was tremulous. "Sounds good."

Her trust humbled him. He didn't want her to ever be afraid, which meant he needed to go slow. Very slow.

"Excellent. So let's enjoy dinner, then." Feeling more confident, he handed over the keys to the valet-parking attendant and escorted Elana upstairs to the plush restaurant overlooking the shores of Lake Michigan.

Elana captured more than one man's gaze as she walked past, but she seemed oblivious to the attention. Their table was small and cozy, with an awesome view of the sunset over the water.

"It's spectacular," Elana murmured, gazing at the rippling waves on the great lake.

"Not nearly as spectacular as you," he said, barely giving the breathtaking view a glance.

She blushed, and he reminded himself to take things slow and easy. There was no rush. He requested a bottle of red wine and was pleased when Elana seemed to enjoy it.

"What made you move to Minneapolis?" she asked, sipping her wine.

"That's where I was matched." She inclined her head, indicating she knew about the match process where every medical student from all the graduating classes went through a complicated system of request-ing their first, second and third choices for residency programs across the country. It was involved, yet seemed to work.

"Because you wanted to do trauma?" she asked.

"Yes, because I wanted to do emergency medicine and trauma. Once I finished my residency in the Twin Cities, I decided to stay on as an attending physician."

She stared at her wine. "So it wasn't a conscious decision on your part to avoid staying here after the accident?"

"I went to medical school here," he reminded her. "No, of course I wasn't avoiding Milwaukee. My family lived here. Joel and I were pretty close despite the age gap. Chicago, Milwaukee and Minneapolis were my top three choices, although not necessarily in that order."

The waiter brought their salads, adding fresh ground pepper with a flourish. They ate in silence for a few minutes.

"I went to college here in Milwaukee too," Elana murmured. "But you probably already knew that."

Warily he nodded. "Yeah, I guessed as much," he said evasively.

She gave him an exasperated look. "Brock, Chloe told me about the scholarship you provided."

He gulped, swallowing a whole cherry tomato and nearly choking in the process. "She did?"

"Yes." Elana paused and then leaned forward. "I don't know what to say. A mere thank-you doesn't seem to be enough."

Her gratitude made him mad. Chloe Jenkins shouldn't have opened her big mouth. "Don't. I never wanted you to know where the money came from. For God's sake, Elana, don't you think it was the least I could do? After everything you went through?"

"No, I think you went above and beyond the call of duty." Elana pushed her empty salad plate away. "Chloe was a lifesaver, but now I owe you a debt of gratitude as well."

"No, you don't." This was exactly why he hadn't wanted her to know. "Gratitude isn't what I want from you, Elana."

She nodded slowly. "I know. But you already have my forgiveness."

His heart stumbled in his chest. He should be grateful, but he wanted more than just her forgiveness. He wanted everything she was willing to give. And more. Yet he needed to step warily.

Elana tilted her head to the side. "Did you see the movie *Pay It Forward*?"

"Yes." He dragged his mind to the present.

"Well, that's what I've decided to do. I have some money saved up, and I've decided to use it to offer a scholarship to someone else. I'd like to give another underprivileged child the chance I had to go to college." Her wistful smile broke his heart. "I'd like to call it the Felicity Schultz Memorial Scholarship."

Stunned, he stared at her. Surely she could use the money for a down payment on a house or towards a new car? But the fact that she wanted to honor her sister, the way he'd tried to do, humbled him. "You're incredible. I think that's a great idea," he managed.

Her smile lit up her face, hitting him with the force of a tsunami. "Thank you. I think so too."

He wanted her. Wanted her so badly, he ached with need. The waiter served the rest of their meal, but Brock couldn't have told anyone what they ate, even though when the waiter took his plate away, it was empty. Every nerve in his body shimmered with amplified desire.

Elana declined dessert, so they left the restaurant shortly thereafter. He'd promised her they'd go slow, but he didn't want to take her home. Not yet.

"I have some wine at home if you'd be willing to come over for a bit. Or I can take you home if you'd rather. It's up to you, Elana."

She bit her lip and hesitated. "I'd like to come over for a bit."

He was startled, fully expecting the opposite. "Are you sure?"

A small smile played along her lips. "I'm sure."

Nearly dizzy with relief, he headed to his place. He pulled into the driveway and then went around to help her from the car. Slow. He was going to take this slow.

Slow would kill him, but better that than scaring her.

Inside, he flicked on a light and gestured to the sofa. "Have a seat. Can I get you something to drink? Wine? Or a soft drink?"

"No, I don't think so." She caught his hand, preventing him from going into the kitchen. "What I'd really like is for you to kiss me again."

Heaven help him, he'd promised to go slow. Yet how

could he keep himself under control when she looked at him like that? Her moist lips were parted softly, inviting him to take her up on the offer.

As if he could do anything else?

"Elana," he whispered, pulling her into his arms and holding her close as if she were the rarest, most fragile vase on earth. He dipped his head, his mouth hovering over hers. "Please be sure."

"I'm sure." She rose up on her tiptoes, closing the space between them to press her mouth to his.

A kaleidoscope of color burst behind his eyelids as her mouth teased his, the tip of her tongue outlining his lips seductively. He kept chanting inwardly, *go slow, go slow*, but the razor edge of desire soon overwhelmed rational thought.

He pulled her against him, deepening the kiss, drowning in the honeyed depths of her mouth. His blood pounded in his chest, but he didn't stop. He'd waited forever for this, and now that he had her in his arms, he didn't want to let go.

She wrapped her arms around his neck, returning his kiss with fervor. Trying not to scare her, yet unable to hold back, he slid his hands beneath her bottom and lifted her higher, so she fit snugly against him.

She let out a moan when he released her mouth and trailed a line of kisses down the side of her neck. As thin as her sexy little red dress was, he was annoyed by the barrier, wanting nothing but her silky soft skin between them.

"Here?" she whispered, and it was then he realized he'd pressed her up against the living room wall.

He realized what he was doing and froze. What was wrong with him? His first time with Elana shouldn't be like this. She deserved better. Far better. Gasping for breath, he desperately tried to control his raging need.

"Hold on," he said gruffly, lifting her higher in his arms and carrying her down the hall to his bedroom.

"I could have walked," she murmured, her breath near his ear causing shivers of awareness.

"Maybe, but this way I don't have to let you go." He tried to smile but failed. He was more serious than he let on. Letting her go wasn't an option. The very idea brought a rush of panic.

One step at a time, he reminded himself. When he reached the edge of his king-sized bed, he let her go so she could stand on her own two feet. He kissed her again, gently this time, enjoying the softness of her mouth.

"Are you sure about this?" he asked, determined to give her one last chance to change her mind.

"Yes."

"And you'll tell me if I do something you don't like?" He couldn't bear the thought of hurting her.

"You won't." She sounded confident.

He wished he felt as much. With the moonlight streaming through his window, he could see a small smile tugging at the corner of her mouth. She lifted her hands and began opening the buttons on his dress shirt, one by one. Her fingers lightly brushed against his skin, making him crazy imagining the possibility of those hands touching him all over.

Going slow was no longer an option. He yanked off his shirt, without giving her time to finish with the buttons. Shucking off his pants, he stood there in a pair of navy boxers, his need evident. When he reached for her dress, she stepped back out of reach and slowly, oh, so slowly, drew the garment off, revealing her silky olive skin and a skimpy red bra and matching thong.

"Elana." He wished he'd turned on a light, so he could see every precious inch of her. He could barely tear his gaze away, frustrated with the inadequacy of mere words. Beautiful. Stunning. Sexy. None of the adjectives he could name came even close to describing her.

"Brock," she echoed, although her teasing smile reassured him. "Come to bed."

Lord knew he wasn't going to make her ask twice.

When Brock carried her into the bedroom, Elana was grateful he'd left the lights off. The room wasn't completely dark, but dark enough that she didn't need to worry about him seeing too much.

Deep down, she could admit she'd chosen the sexy red dress just for this reason. Brock had only seen her wearing scrubs or jeans. She'd wanted to look nice for him. Attractive. Sexy.

Considering her lack of experience, she was hoping the dress would give her the courage to seduce him.

The shadowy moonlight gave her the boldness to

strip down to her underwear, and she reveled in his stark, hungry gaze. Seconds later they were naked.

She pushed aside the brief flash of vulnerability. She hadn't been with a man for a long time, but she wasn't nervous with Brock. Not any more. This was exactly where she wanted to be. The bed was soft beneath her, and the sheets smelled like him, musky and male.

He lavished kisses along her breasts, and she thought she was going to lose her mind. Her nipples peaked, begging for more. He lightly stroked them with his tongue, but then he trailed kisses down her abdomen to the inside of her thighs, and she knew she wasn't going to survive.

She whimpered when he parted her thighs and pressed his mouth there, where no man had ever kissed her before. She cried out, her hips bucking off the bed as her orgasm hit hard. Brock didn't stop, though he took his time, loving her, kissing her and rekindling her desire.

"Brock, please," she begged as she wrapped her legs around his waist.

"Shh, we have all night," he promised. But he did grab a condom, and after sheathing himself, he settled between her legs and probed her opening.

She was ready. More than ready. It seemed she'd waited her entire life for him.

"Now. Please." Her impatience made him chuckle, but when he finally granted her wish and slid deep, neither one of them was laughing.

Intense, sensational pleasure filled her body, her nerve endings tingling even as she strained against him, seeking more. And this time, when her orgasm took her sailing over the edge, Brock was right there with her.

She held his head to her breast when he collapsed against her, his harsh breathing audible over the roaring of her pulse. Shaken, she stared at the ceiling.

No man had ever loved her the way Brock just had. And she was very much afraid she'd never be satisfied with anything less than the intense closeness they'd just shared.

CHAPTER TWELVE

ELANA lost track of how many times Brock made love to her throughout the rest of the night. Each time surprisingly better, tender and yet more intense than the last.

He held her close, even while they were asleep. She'd always preferred to keep her own personal space around her, but, somehow, with Brock, she didn't mind so much. Even more amazing, she found she was able to fall asleep despite his heavy weight pressing against her.

When the morning light streamed in through Brock's bedroom window, she swallowed a groan and stretched her aching muscles. The bright light of day brought her old insecurities to the surface, so she quietly slid from his bed, trying not to disturb him.

Feeling acutely self-conscious, she picked up his shirt, thankful it covered her down to her knees. She made her way quietly to his bathroom.

Emerging a few minutes later, she searched for her dress, wishing she'd brought along some comfy, casual clothes to wear. Brock's cell phone rang loudly, startling her so badly she let out a high-pitched squeak.

"What are you doing?" Brock asked sleepily, ignoring his cell phone as he stared at her. "Sneaking out on me?"

"No, I was going to cook something for breakfast." She felt a little guilty because she had, for a split second, considered sneaking out on him. His cell phone continued to ring. "You'd better answer that," she said, gesturing to the phone while still holding the wrinkled red dress in front of her. "What if it's Lacey or, what's his name, Rufus?"

Brock muttered a curse under his breath and dug in his discarded pants for his phone. It had stopped ringing by the time he grabbed it. He stared at the screen. "I can't believe it. I missed Joel's call."

The sheet pooled at his waist as he punched Redial. She had trouble keeping her gaze off his chest as he waited for Joel to answer. "Joel? I'm so glad you called. I've been looking all over for you. Are you all right? Where are you?"

Elana held her breath, blatantly listening to Brock's side of the conversation with his missing brother.

"Yeah, I know things have been rough," Brock said, scrubbing a hand over his jaw as he talked. "Tucker needs you, Joel. You were right: his crying was an indication of something more. He's in the hospital, being treated for pneumonia." There was another pause as Joel said something.

"Yeah, don't worry. He's doing better, I swear. I wouldn't lie to you, Joel."

Elana edged closer, wishing she could hear what Joel was saying. "Is Lacey with him?" she whispered.

"Joel, listen, Tucker needs you. Hurry home, okay?

No, don't hang up! Dammit!" Brock stared at his phone in dismay. "I can't believe he just did that."

"What? Where is he? Is Lacey with him?"

"No, Lacey isn't with him. He told me he's tried to call her, but she didn't answer her phone. He said to tell her he loves her and that he'll be back soon." Brock's tone was laced with helplessness. "I didn't get a chance to tell him Lacey disappeared too."

"You could try calling him back."

"No. He's in Pelican Point. One of his buddies got him an interview with a home remodeling company that pays better than what he used to make at the gas station."

"Well, that's progress." Elana sank down onto the bed beside Brock.

"Yeah. Progress." He let out a heavy sigh. "I only wish he would have told me his plans before he took off. At the very least, he should have told Lacey."

"He wasn't thinking clearly, I'm sure. He was probably feeling trapped," Elana said, relieved that they'd at least heard from Joel. Now if only they knew where Lacey was, things would be back to normal.

"No kidding." Brock's tone was dry.

"He needed a break, and then when he realized he couldn't simply run away from his problems, decided to look for a better paying job," Elana rationalized.

"You're right." Brock grinned, obviously in a better mood now that he'd heard from his brother. "He promised to call me back in a few days once he finds out for sure about this home remodeling job. Says the owner is willing to make him some sort of apprentice."

An apprentice sounded promising.

"Do you think he and Lacey will move to Pelican Point?" She knew Brock would miss Tucker if that happened.

"I don't know. Maybe. I could help them find a place, get them settled so they're not starting out too financially in debt. Or they could commute for a while, until they save up for a house."

Brock to the rescue. Again. First her scholarship, then getting himself through medical school, and now supporting his brother and his nephew. She leaned forward and gave him a quick kiss. "I'm glad Joel called. See? You didn't need that private investigator after all. And I bet Lacey will be back soon too."

He pulled her close, returning her kiss with passion. "Now I remember where we were before my brother rudely interrupted us," he murmured between kisses.

She was tempted to give in and crawl back into bed with him. Yet she was worried about her scars. And she hadn't been lying earlier. She was really hungry. Must be all the calories they'd burned throughout the night.

"Where are you going?" he complained when she pulled away. He held on to her hand, refusing to let go.

She grinned. "I promised to make you breakfast, didn't I? I always keep my promises."

"Wearing only my shirt?" he asked with a frankly hopeful gaze.

She let out a wry chuckle. "Well, it's either your shirt or my dress, since that's all I have." Elana stood and turned away, draping her dress over the bottom of the bed. She'd wait to change until after she'd had a chance to eat. Maybe then she'd borrow Brock's shower.

"Hurry up," she added as she walked away, buttoning up his shirt. "Because I'm hungry enough to eat your portion too."

"You wouldn't be that cruel," he protested. After a few minutes, she heard the water running in the bathroom.

No, she wouldn't be that cruel. She smiled and hummed to herself as she gathered the ingredients to make French toast.

So this was how it felt to be happy.

Brock used the bathroom and then hurried out to share breakfast with Elana.

"Smells wonderful," he said, pleased that she'd made the effort to cook for him. Not that he thought it was a woman's job. Far from it. He'd taught himself to cook years ago. "Thanks, Elana."

"You're welcome," she said in a muffled voice. There was only half a piece of French toast left on her plate, and a surplus of syrup indicated she'd already eaten her share.

"You're amazing. I like a woman with a hearty appetite." He helped himself to several slices of French toast and took the seat across from her. The way she looked, wearing nothing but his white dress shirt, the dusky tips of her breasts visible through the cotton fabric, made him hungry for something other than food.

The night they'd shared had been amazing. He wanted nothing more than to spend the rest of the day with her.

"How many more would you like?" Elana asked,

getting up from the table and going over to the electric frying pan.

"This is enough for me, thanks."

She frowned at him over her shoulder. "Something wrong with my cooking?"

"Of course not, you went above and beyond making breakfast." How could he explain he was too keyed up about having her in his home to eat? "I should have cooked for you."

"Next time," Elana murmured.

"Absolutely," he agreed, thrilled at the thought of there being a next time. He couldn't deny he was feeling very possessive where she was concerned.

"You've mentioned your dad a few times," Elana said as she returned to her seat across from him at the table. "But you haven't mentioned your mother."

His family. Of course Elana wanted to talk about his family. A chunk of French toast lodged in his throat, and he swallowed with an effort. "That's because she passed away my first year of medical school."

"I'm sorry, Brock." Elana's empathetic expression made him feel ashamed. After everything she'd been through, his family issues were nothing. "I'm guessing your father didn't handle it very well."

He lifted a shoulder in a careless shrug. "Dad was always the disciplinarian of the house. Believe it or not, I was the one who tended to follow the rules. Joel, on the other hand, rebelled."

"You were close," she guessed.

He nodded. "After Mom died, I think things between

my dad and my brother got even worse. I felt bad I couldn't be there for Joel when he needed me."

"I can imagine." Elana stared down at her plate for a minute. "Give him a chance, Brock. He'll come around."

"I know." His brother had more of a chance of coming around than his father did. "Tucker's crying really bothered Joel. I'm sure he took off because he was afraid of turning out like our father."

Elana sucked in a harsh breath. "Are you saying— your father hit you?"

"Not really," he answered honestly. "But he did use his tongue as a weapon, saying hurtful things." He didn't go into detail, trying to shelter her as best he could. "I often wondered why my mother stayed and put up with him."

"Maybe she loved him," Elana said, her troubled gaze meeting his. "Maybe she loved you and your brother too much to leave."

His gut clenched, and he automatically shook his head. "I don't understand that kind of love."

"I do."

He snapped his head up to look at her in surprise.

Elana continued in a low voice. "I was a sullen, angry teenager, but Chloe still loved me. And I thank God every day for bringing her into my life."

He winced, realizing the extent of his blunder. "I'm sorry, Elana. You're right—"

"I'm going to take a shower," she interrupted. "Excuse me."

She stood and practically ran from the room,

taking the mangled mess of his heart with her. For a moment all he could do was to curse at himself under his breath.

What was wrong with him? Why didn't he learn to think before he spoke?

Elana would surely leave now that he'd insulted her.

Suddenly, he couldn't bear the idea. He wasn't going to let her go. Not without a fight. Maybe he was an idiot, opening his mouth and blabbing about things he didn't know anything about, but he could learn.

He loved her. The realization hit him, hard.

He loved her!

Shaky, he splayed his hands on the table. Okay, he loved her. That didn't mean Elana was ready to hear the truth about his feelings. They'd only just made love.

But he could show her, with actions rather than words.

He wolfed down the rest of his breakfast and then hovered for a moment outside the bathroom door. Images of a naked Elana in the shower tortured him, but, somehow, he knew this wasn't the time or the place to encroach on her personal space.

He told himself to leave her alone. To wait until she was finished, but then the shower turned off, and a few seconds later he heard a yelp and a loud thud.

"Elana?" He opened the door a crack. When he saw her lying on the floor, her face drawn in pain as she clutched her knee, he didn't hesitate but barged the rest of the way in. "What happened?"

"I was stupid. I reached for the towel, slipped on a wet spot in the floor, and jammed my knee." She leaned against the sink, clutching a towel to her chest. He didn't have the heart to tell her the small cloth didn't provide much cover.

"Let me see," he said, dropping to his knees to examine her. Her skin was silky soft, and he found it difficult to concentrate. He focused on the swollen spot on her knee. "We need some ice. This is going to bruise."

"I hope it doesn't get to the point I can't work."

He traced the swollen area carefully. "It feels superficial." This close to the front of her thighs, he noticed the scars. Numerous thin white lines, about an inch long, running in parallel lines up the surface of both legs.

Puzzled, he ran his finger up the length of her leg. Glancing up, he saw similar scars on her arms. Had she been in an accident too? "My God, Elana. What on earth happened to you?"

She froze, her muscles going stiff. At first he didn't understand the significance, but then she jerked away from him, nearly giving herself another vicious bruise as she leaped over him in her haste to reach the door.

"Elana?" The cold air was nothing like the icy fist of sheer panic that squeezed his heart. "What is it? What's wrong?"

Seeing the tortured expression in her eyes moments before she bolted from the bathroom, he suddenly understood. Mentally, he smacked himself for being so stupid.

She'd known about Lacey's cutting herself, in a desperate need for control, because Elana had done the same thing.

Those thin, faint scars on her skin were evidence of her self-inflicted cuts.

* * *

How could she have forgotten her scars?

Limping, she ran into Brock's bedroom and swiped the towel over her body before tossing it aside. She grabbed her dress, her fingers shaking so bad she nearly dropped it.

With a determined yank, she pulled the wrinkled fabric over her head, without bothering to track down her undergarments.

She had to get out of here. Now.

Where were her shoes?

Her stomach lurched, and she had to swallow hard to keep from throwing up the French toast she'd eaten. Her shoes were on opposite sides of the room, and after she found them both, she jammed her feet into the ridiculously high-heeled pumps, wincing as the stupid shoes made her knee hurt worse, and headed for the door.

Only to stop abruptly, completely horrified to see Brock standing there, blocking her means of escape.

"Elana, please wait." He stood there, his expression anguished. "Don't go."

She momentarily closed her eyes, wishing she could just disappear, that this nightmare would be over. But she knew clicking her ruby heels together wasn't going to work to get her home. Gathering every ounce of self-control, she opened her eyes and struggled to find her voice. "Move out of my way."

He didn't budge. "I caused this to happen to you?" he asked hoarsely, his gaze full of self-recrimination.

His fingers were clenched into white-knuckled fists. "I did this?"

No matter how mortified she was that he'd discovered the truth, she couldn't let him take the blame. He hadn't shied away from her scars in horror.

He was taking responsibility for them.

But they weren't his fault. Not really. Chloe had made sure she'd known she wasn't the only kid in the world to be dealt a lousy hand. What a person did with the cards they'd been given was no one's fault but their own.

She knew that now.

She forced herself to meet his gaze. "No. I did this to myself."

CHAPTER THIRTEEN

"I'M SORRY," Brock murmured, venturing closer, his expression still tortured. "I'm so sorry."

If he kept apologizing like this, she was going to lose it. She angled her chin, desperately trying to hang on to her anger, to remain strong. "I already told you it's not your fault. Please, just let me go."

"I can't." Brock remained exactly where he stood, still blocking the doorway leading out of his bedroom. "Not like this."

What did he want from her? Blood? A touch of hysteria bubbled in her chest. "Why not? My ugly scars have nothing to do with you."

"They're not ugly, Elana. I hate knowing you suffered, but those scars are not ugly." His gaze narrowed in anger. "Who told you they were? Some idiot past lover?"

She resented how he seemed to read her so easily, and she lifted a shoulder in a careless shrug. "Doesn't matter. I know they're ugly. I see the evidence every day."

"Yet you hide them from the rest of the world," he

said in a low voice. "Wearing long sleeves beneath your scrubs. Why didn't you say anything to me about them?" Brock took another step into the room, his imploring gaze eroding the edges of her resistance. "After expressing your concerns about Lacey, why didn't you tell me what happened to you?"

What happened to her? As if her scars were some sort of bizarre accident, rather than the intentional self-mutilation she knew them to be? "I'm not proud of what I did to myself, Brock. Do you have any idea how difficult it's been for me to pull my life back together?"

"I can only imagine, and knowing what you've accomplished only makes me respect you more." His tone was firm, and a tiny part of her longed to believe.

But respect? Hardly. He had no idea.

"I know you're a strong woman, Elana," he continued. "You've shown me your strength in a variety of ways, not least of which the way you volunteer your time to take care of others." His brows pulled together in a puzzled frown. "You're the strongest woman I've ever known, which is why I don't understand why you believe those scars are something to be ashamed of."

Obviously, he didn't get it. Didn't understand the burden she carried. And she was finished talking about this. "I'm going home, Brock. Move out of my way."

"Elana, please, don't do this. Don't throw away what we shared last night."

"We had sex last night," she said bluntly. Wonderful, glorious sex—at least that's how she thought of it until he'd noticed her scars and all her old insecurities had rushed back. "Because I wanted to."

A flicker of uncertainty flashed in his eyes, and she squashed a niggle of self-doubt for downplaying the closeness they'd shared. "It was more than sex for me," he said slowly. "We made love. All night long."

Her mouth went dry. He didn't mean that. Not really.

Brock's gaze grew fierce. "Did you hear what I said, Elana? What we shared was making love. I love you. Scars and all, I love you."

He loved her? No, she didn't believe it. He couldn't be serious. "You don't know what you're saying."

"Yes, I do. I love you." He took another step forward, and she immediately backed away. "Please don't leave. Stay. Talk to me."

How could he love her? He was only saying that because he didn't really understand. Didn't know the darkness that had haunted her for so long.

"We've been talking," she protested, suddenly weary. "Talking isn't going to change anything. You're only saying all this because you feel bad. Because you think you're somehow responsible for these scars. But you're not. What can I say to convince you?"

"You could stay. You could let me hold you." He reached out towards her.

Flinching from his touch, she shook her head. If he touched her, held her, she'd lose what little control she had left. "Look, this isn't personal. I just need a little time, some space."

"It's not personal? I tell you I love you, and you think

this isn't personal?" For the first time, a note of anger tinted his tone. "Hell, I hate to tell you, but having you walk away from me feels pretty damn personal, Elana."

She'd hurt him, even though she hadn't meant to. She remembered what Chloe had asked: if she was worried she might be the one to hurt him. Yet she was the one with the scars. With the horrible past. None of this was making any sense.

She just wanted some time alone. To think. To try to figure things out.

His phone rang again, and she glanced at the device clipped to the waistband of his jeans. "Aren't you going to get that?"

Stubbornly he shook his head. "They'll call back, I'm sure."

"What if it's Lacey this time?"

He glanced down, uncertainty shadowing his gaze.

"She'll think you're mad at her if you ignore her."

He muttered a curse under his breath. "I'll talk to her later. Right now, I think it's best if I do take you home."

She'd almost forgotten she didn't have her car. She almost insisted on taking a taxi but didn't want to hurt Brock any more than she already had by refusing something as simple as a ride. She gave a jerky nod. "Fine."

When he disappeared into the living room, she quickly searched for her undergarments. Changing fast, she took off the dress, put on her bra and underwear, and then pulled her dress back on.

Being properly dressed made her feel better. She

headed out to the living room, forcing herself to sit on the edge of the sofa to wait.

Brock emerged from the kitchen, his phone in his hand, his expression wary.

"What's wrong?" she asked, suddenly worried. She jumped to her feet. "Lacey? Has something happened to Lacey?"

"No, this was the pediatrician from Children's Memorial. Tucker is ready to be discharged."

"Oh." She relaxed a bit. "That's good news."

He grimaced. "It's good for Tucker, but I'm going to need help, Elana. How am I going to care for a baby on my own without Lacey? I've always avoided kids. I know it's a lot to ask, but will you help me?" Deep down, he knew he could have just hired a nanny, but what he really wanted was Elana.

Help him? She couldn't. He was asking too much of her.

So then why hadn't she told him no?

Elana rode with Brock to the hospital to pick up Tucker, telling herself that she'd help him get things settled with the baby at home before she left.

While he was driving, he tossed his phone at her. "Try Lacey again, would you?"

She opened his phone and found Lacey's number. Lacey's cell phone went straight to voice mail.

"No answer," she said, snapping his phone shut.

His mouth tightened, but he didn't say anything.

She wanted to reassure him that Lacey would be back, that she'd return his car and step up to take care of her son, but, at this point, words were useless. The longer Lacey stayed away, the worse things looked. She knew only too well how the inevitable darkness could warp a person's perceptions.

She hoped and prayed Lacey was okay.

Wordlessly, they took the elevators up to the sixth floor. Entering Tucker's room, they found the nurse in with him.

"I'm glad you're here," she said in relief, thrusting the baby at Brock. "I wanted to get this little guy discharged before my next patient came in."

Brock held Tucker in his arms, only the tiniest hint of panic in his gaze. "He's finished with his IV antibiotics?" he asked, noting the absence of an IV.

"Yes, we switched him to oral meds this morning, and he seems to be doing fine. The doctor said you should continue the oral antibiotics for another week. Really, he shouldn't have any other problems; he's been an angel."

"Well, he doesn't seem to be crying much," Brock murmured.

Elana crossed over to pick up the diaper bag Lacey must have left and slung the strap over her shoulder.

Brock held Tucker as the nurse rattled on about the last time he'd eaten. She couldn't tear her gaze from Brock. The enthralled expression on his face, as he gently stroked a finger down Tucker's cheek, hit her low in the stomach, stealing her breath.

Brock couldn't have looked any more natural if Tucker were his own son. And in that moment, she caught a glimpse of the future. A tiny shred of hope.

The family she'd always dreamed about.

* * *

Gently, so as not to wake him, Brock lifted Tucker and set him in his infant car seat, bypassing his quilted jacket, since the day was warm and sunny. After buckling Tucker into the seat, he covered the car seat with a blanket, the way he'd watched Lacey do.

He cast a glance at Elana, knowing he'd pushed his luck by asking her to stay and help him.

It was the only thing he could think of that might convince her to stay. She would stay for Lacey's sake. And maybe for Tucker's.

But not his. And certainly not for herself.

"Here's the prescription," the nurse said, shoving a slip of paper at him. "You can get this filled at any pharmacy. And all the rest of Tucker's discharge instructions are on this sheet here."

Clearly, the nurse was eager to be on her way. He couldn't totally blame her, since she did mention having a new admission.

"Thanks. I'm sure we'll be fine."

Elana shot a surprised glance at him but didn't say anything.

He lifted the infant carrier and gestured to the door. "Ready?" he asked. "We can stop at a drugstore on the way home."

He imagined she flinched when he said the word *home*. He had to swallow hard to stop himself from making a bigger fool of himself than he already had. He'd told Elana that he loved her.

Clearly she didn't believe him.

And he had no way of knowing what to say to convince her.

Elana didn't say much, other than offering to stay in the car with the baby while he ran into the local pharmacy to pick up Tucker's liquid antibiotics.

The minute he carried Tucker inside the house, though, the baby woke up and began to cry.

"Hey, what's wrong?" he said in alarm as he unbuckled the baby from his car seat. "You were doing so much better."

Elana watched from the doorway, as if she were just waiting for the right moment to leave. And suddenly he realized he shouldn't try to make her stay. Taking advantage of her innate kindness.

He'd only wanted another chance to talk to her. To make her understand what he was barely able to comprehend himself.

How much he loved her. And how together they really had a chance of making things work.

But if Tucker was going to keep crying, they weren't going to have any time alone. And his tiny nephew was his problem, not hers.

"Elana, you don't have to stay; we'll be fine."

"Are you sure?" The deep furrows in her brow indicated she wasn't convinced. When Tucker continued to wail, she pushed away from the door. "I'll make a bottle of formula for you to try. Maybe he's hungry."

She disappeared into the kitchen before he could protest. He walked around the living room in a feeble attempt to get Tucker to calm down. When she came back, she handed him a warmed bottle, so he awkwardly sat on the end of the sofa and tried to get Tucker to eat.

He wasn't interested. In seconds he was crying again.

"Here, let me try."

He handed over the baby, and Elana must have had some sort of magic touch, because Tucker settled down to suck on his bottle.

"How did you do that?" he muttered.

"I don't know. Maybe he could tell you weren't comfortable with him." She smiled down at Tucker, bending to gently kiss his head.

Lucky Tucker to be in Elana's arms. He wished more than anything he'd handled things differently that morning. But he hadn't. God help him, he'd never once thought she'd inflicted those cuts herself.

He took a deep breath and tried to concentrate on the matter at hand. Tucker. Soon he'd be alone with Tucker.

"He'd better get used to me," he said with a frown. "Because right now, I'm all he's got."

Elana glanced up at him, her expression troubled. "What if Lacey doesn't come back? Do you think Joel will still come back to take over?"

He couldn't hide the flash of panic in his eyes. "I don't know. Maybe."

Her gaze clouded with doubt. He couldn't blame her. The way Joel had taken off in the first place made him doubt his brother too.

"Maybe I was wrong, Brock," Elana said, smoothing a hand over Tucker's head. "I've been thinking we should call the police. What if something happened to Lacey, like a car accident or something worse?"

He stared at her for a minute. "Don't you think we would hear about it if she was in a car crash?"

"Not if no one's found her and she's too sick to make a phone call." Elana's brow puckered in a frown. "Call the police. Tell them how Lacey took off. Report your car stolen."

He was shocked at her sudden turn of heart. "Elana, don't you think that will make things worse for Lacey?"

Elana turned away, burying her face against Tucker. "I don't know," she said in a muffled yet agonized voice.

He understood what she was really afraid of. Elana carried scars just like Lacey's. She knew better than anyone what was going on in Lacey's troubled mind. "You don't think she's coming back."

She lifted her head to look at him, her gaze full of desperate fear. "I'm not sure. And I'm afraid that if your brother knows she's gone, then he might not come back either. And then what will happen?"

Taking the bottle from Tucker's mouth, she sat him in her lap and rubbed his back until he burped. He looked away from his nephew's sweet, innocent face, his chest tightening.

"They'll be back." He wished he sounded more convincing.

"What if they don't come back?" she persisted. "What would happen to Tucker? Would you adopt him? Give him the loving home and family he needs?"

Brock swallowed hard, unable to respond. He knew

he should tell her what she wanted to hear, but he couldn't. Just the thought of raising a child made him feel sick to his stomach.

He'd already stolen one young woman's life. And look what had happened to Elana. The scars weren't the worst of it, he knew. They were only a reminder of how she'd been through hell and back.

No, he couldn't do it.

And suddenly he realized that loving Elana wasn't enough. He didn't have anything to offer. Not if she had her heart and soul set on having a family.

Elana felt her heart squeeze painfully in her chest when she saw the stricken look in Brock's eyes. Not wanting children was one thing, but to give up Tucker? No, she couldn't believe it. "You'd give him up to strangers?" she asked in a hoarse whisper.

"It won't come to that," he said finally, sidestepping her question. He looked away, avoiding her gaze as he gestured to Lacey's room. "The portable crib is still set up in there if you'd like to put him down."

"Sure." Regretfully, she carried the baby to Lacey's room, leaving the light off and only using the illumination from the hallway to find the crib.

She carefully set him down on his back, covering his body with a blanket. He stirred a bit but didn't wake up. She stared at him for a long minute, thinking he was the most beautiful baby she'd ever seen.

How could Brock even think of giving him up? Inwardly reeling, she tried to comprehend what was going through his mind. What had he said earlier? He'd always avoided kids? Did he seriously plan to live the rest of his life without children?

Sure he did. Because all this time he had lived his life only for his patients. He'd never planned on having a future of his own.

He couldn't love her. He couldn't possibly love her if he thought she wouldn't one day want to have babies of her own.

She heard the muffled thud of a car door slamming shut.

Visitors? With a curious frown, she walked back out to the living room to find Brock opening up the front door.

"Lacey!" Brock exclaimed in relief. "I'm so glad you're back."

"Where is he?" Lacey barely spared Brock a glance, searching the room frantically for her son. "Where's Tucker?"

"I just put him down in the crib," Elana said, trying to reassure Lacey. "He's fine, doing great, in fact. We just picked him up from the hospital today."

"I need to see him," Lacey said, quickly heading for the bedroom.

Elana glanced at Brock.

The relief in his eyes was starkly overwhelming.

Lacey was back and obviously planned to take over Tucker's care.

There was no reason for her to stay.

CHAPTER FOURTEEN

"Tucker is really doing better?" Lacey asked, coming back into the room.

Elana forced a smile. "Actually, he is a lot better. Has hardly cried at all since the antibiotics have started working on curing the pneumonia."

"I'm glad." Lacey looked relieved.

"Where in the heck have you been?" Brock demanded.

"I went home to see my mother," Lacey admitted. "Obviously, you probably guessed I haven't been home in a long time. In almost two years, to be exact. I don't much care for my stepfather, but my mom seemed glad to see me."

"I'm proud of you for going, Lacey." Elana reached out to gently touch her arm. "I'm sure that must have been difficult."

Lacey shrugged, but Elana could tell the visit home hadn't been casual or easy. "She wants to meet Tucker and Joel sometime, and maybe I'll arrange for her to come visit without my stepfather." She glanced glumly around Brock's house. "I guess Joel hasn't been back yet, huh?"

"He called this morning, actually," Brock said with a reassuring smile. "Wanted me to tell you he loves you and that he's hoping to land a new job as an apprentice for a home remodeling company."

"Really?" Lacey's eyes brightened. "He said he loved me?"

"I swear." He crossed his heart and cocked an eyebrow. "Maybe if you'd turned on your cell phone, he would have called you directly."

Lacey flushed. "I know. I'm sorry. I forgot my cell phone battery charger here. I guess I was just so desperate to get away." She looked uncomfortable, as if remembering their argument in the cafeteria.

"You're here now, Lacey, and that's all that matters," Elana pointed out.

"I missed Tucker so much," Lacey admitted, her eyes glimmering with a hint of tears. "More than I thought I would. When I went to the hospital and saw some strange baby in Tucker's room, I freaked out. It took a while for the nurse to calm me down enough to let me know you guys had brought him home."

As much as Elana wanted to leave, had in fact edged closer to the doorway, she couldn't just abandon Lacey. She put a comforting arm around the young mother's slim shoulders. "It's okay. Everything is going to be just fine."

Lacey hugged Elana back, but her gaze was still centered on Brock. "My mom gave me some money; it's not a lot but enough to hold me over until Joel comes home."

"Lacey, don't worry about the money. That's not what's important." Brock's gaze momentarily dropped to her forearms. "You are what matters. I'm willing to help in any way I can."

Lacey must have noticed his gaze because her chin came up a notch. "You were right; I have been cutting myself. It started a long time ago, for reasons that don't matter any more. But I'm getting better. I haven't cut myself in over a week. I'm trying to be a good mother to Tucker."

Elana was amazed Lacey blurted out the truth like that. "No one ever said you weren't a good mother, Lacey," Elana hastened to point out.

"Of course not. I was just worried about you," Brock added lamely. His alarmed gaze collided with Elana's, practically begging her for help and guidance in handling Lacey's revelation.

She swallowed hard, wondering what she was supposed to say. She was hardly an expert.

Yet suddenly she understood exactly what she needed to do.

"Lacey, I want to show you something." Elana stepped away, slowly pulling up the long sleeves of her dress, exposing her arms. "I know exactly what you're going through. Because I used to cut myself too."

"You did?" Lacey's eyes widened with undisguised amazement. She reached out to tentatively stroke the telltale raised ridges of Elana's scars. "Just like me?"

She nodded. The scars weren't exactly badges of honor, but in a way they were a sign of hope. Of healing. "Just like you. For reasons that don't matter any more to me, either. But you can beat it, Lacey. I learned to stop, and I have all the confidence in the world you can too."

"I hope so," Lacey said in an awed and somewhat hesitant tone. "I really hope so."

"I'll help you," Elana offered. "Anything you need, ask me. In fact, if you start feeling desperate, like you need to cut yourself, call me. I'll come whenever I can, and we'll talk it through."

"Is that how you stopped?" Lacey asked.

Her throat swelled with emotion as she remembered Chloe's loving support. Because as strange as it might sound, using the sharp edge of a razor, and making tiny slices in your skin despite the pain, was as addictive as any narcotic. The cycle had been extremely difficult to break. "Yes. I had help too, from Chloe. She was my foster mother. She took me in after I ran away from several other foster homes."

"I don't think my mother would understand at all, but I'm glad to know you went through this too." Lacey's smile warmed her heart. "It's a deal. I'll call you if I need help kicking the habit."

Elana couldn't help wondering about Lacey's mother. If Lacey had been her daughter, she would have moved heaven and earth to bring her daughter and grandson home. But at least Lacey wasn't alone any more.

She'd be there for Lacey, no matter what happened between her and Brock.

Lacey turned to Brock, who was watching them intently. "I hope you're not too upset with me for leaving."

"No, of course not," he said gruffly. "We were worried something bad had happened to you, that's all."

Lacey slowly nodded. "I know. And for that I'm sorry."

"Are you hungry?" Brock asked, changing the subject. His gaze included Elana. "How about I order out for some pizza?"

This was her cue to leave. "None for me, thanks. I really need to get going."

"Won't you stay?" His gaze clung to hers.

"No, thanks. I have some things I really need to do." She cared about Brock. Cared about Lacey and Tucker too. But she didn't believe in Brock's love. She wasn't even sure he knew how to love.

Lacey was here, and Tucker would be fine.

It was well past time to go home.

Elana tried to ignore the shrill ringing of her phone, the third call within five minutes. Brock's number lit up the face of her phone. Again. Part of her knew she was being childish in refusing to answer, but, truthfully, she wasn't sure what to say.

She'd spent a restless night, tossing and turning, so she wasn't in the best frame of mind. She'd ignored his calls all morning. Was dreading going in to work and seeing him. Working with him as if they were nothing but colleagues.

While her heart ached with wanting the impossible.

When Lacey's number lit up her screen almost an hour later, she didn't consider ignoring the call. Considering how she'd promised to be there for Lacey, she quickly pressed the button to answer. "Hi, Lacey, what's up?"

"Why aren't you answering Brock's phone calls?" she asked in exasperation. "He's driving me crazy, constantly asking me to call you."

Elana sighed. She should have figured Brock would know her well enough to know she wouldn't ignore Lacey's call. "Brock has no right to drag you into our mess."

"I know you didn't ask for my opinion, but I think he's freaking out over your scars," Lacey confided in a low tone. "The look on his face yesterday when you pulled up your sleeves…" Her voice trailed off.

Elana glanced down at her bare arms. It felt weird not to have long sleeves on. She was trying to work up the courage to go to work wearing only her short-sleeved scrubs, but she wasn't sure she could do it. "No, that's not it. Brock has already seen my scars." Her laugh held a trace of bitterness. "Every single one of them."

"All of them?" Lacey echoed. Then her tone changed as she put the obvious two and two together. "Oh, I see. Well, then, what's the problem with you two?"

"It's a long story," Elana said evasively. "And I'd rather not get into it, if you don't mind."

There was a brief pause, and Elana knew she'd hurt Lacey's feelings when she said, "Sure. Whatever."

She closed her eyes, burning with shame. Lacey was trying to be a friend; she deserved better than that. "Lacey, I'm sorry. If you want to know what's going on, here it is. Brock claims he loves me, but I don't believe him."

"Do you think he can't love you because of your scars?" Lacey asked.

How could she explain something she didn't fully understand herself? "No, he says he loves me scars and all."

"But you don't believe him?" Lacey persisted.

"No. I have reason to believe he doesn't really know how to love someone." She didn't want to mention to Lacey how she'd asked him about adopting Tucker. She didn't think Lacey would take too kindly to Brock's hesitation.

"Hmm. Well, maybe he has some scars too," Lacey said. "Scars you can't see."

What? The truth hit her like a cement block falling on her head. Of course Brock had scars. Deeply hidden scars. Scars that weren't visible to the naked eye.

Lacey was right. She wasn't being fair to him. "Lacey, you're a genius."

"I am?" Disbelief laced her tone.

"Yes. Ah, look, tell Brock I'll talk to him later." If she was going to talk to Brock, she'd rather talk to him in person, not on the phone.

"All right. At least that should make him happy. Take care, Elana." Lacey disconnected from the line.

Elana let the phone slip from her fingers as she stared blindly out the window.

She'd expected Brock to love her in spite of her scars, the undeniable evidence of her troubled past, but she hadn't been willing to do the same for him.

Because she did love him. Had loved him from the

moment he'd tried to take responsibility for her scars, rather than seeing them as ugly marks of failure.

But she'd done the exact opposite, by making her love for him conditional on having babies.

Brock tossed aside the cell phone he'd been using to call Elana. It was no use. He'd left half a dozen messages, but she wasn't calling him back.

He was going to have to see her in person. The moment she'd walked out of his life, he'd realized the depth of his mistake.

He needed to fix things in a hurry.

His front door opened before he'd reached for the handle. "Joel?"

"Hi, Brock. Are Lacey and Tucker here?"

"Yes, I think Lacey's feeding the baby in the spare bedroom." He gave his brother a slap on the back. "Glad you're home, but I have to go and see Elana."

"Elana? Who's Elana?" Joel asked, exasperated. "Don't you want to hear about my job?"

"You got it?" Joel flashed a wide grin. "Hey, good for you. I'm proud of you, Joel. Look, I promise we'll talk more later."

"Wait a minute," Joel said as Brock continued out the door. "Who's Elana?"

"Ask Lacey," he tossed over his shoulder just before he let the door slam shut behind him.

He headed straight for Elana's apartment building, mentally rehearsing what he wanted to say. When he got to the door, Elana came barreling out, practically running into him, much like the day she'd come running out of her mother's nursing home. Only this time she wasn't crying.

He wasn't sure if that was good or bad. Had she really already made up her mind about him? Deciding he wasn't worth her time and effort?

"Brock!" Elana clasped a hand over her heart. "You scared me."

"I'm sorry," Brock apologized quickly. "I'm glad I caught you, though. Do you have a minute to talk?"

She surprised him by nodding. "Sure. As a matter of fact, I was just going to drive over to see you."

She was? Good. That was really good. Wasn't it? Maybe not. "Do you want to go inside or take a walk?"

After a moment's hesitation, she gestured to the apartment building. "We can go inside."

He followed her back up the stairs and into her apartment. Nervously, he sat on her sofa. Her living room was all warm colors and earth tones.

"You're wearing short sleeves," he said, noticing her attire.

She flushed as she glanced down at her bare arms. "Yes, I'm sort of practicing. I'm not sure if I'm brave enough to go to work this way, but I thought I'd give it a try."

Her admission humbled him. "Elana, I think you're the bravest woman I've ever met."

"Me?" Her eyes widened, and she instantly shook her head. "No, I'm not brave. In fact, that's why I told Lacey I'd talk to you. I wanted a chance to explain."

"Lacey?" Brock looked confused. "You spoke to Lacey?"

"Yes. She told me you asked her to call me."

"Yeah, but she refused." Brock let out a low chuckle. "She must have called you anyway. I guess I owe her a debt of gratitude if something she said made you change your mind about talking to me."

Elana sat down beside him, her gaze serious. "She did. I need to tell you that I'm sorry. I shouldn't have gotten so upset when you didn't seem thrilled to adopt Tucker."

"Please, Elana, let me explain." Brock reached over to take her hand. "You were right that day. I've made dedicating my life to saving patients more important than having a life of my own. To be honest, in some warped way, I didn't think I deserved to raise a child. Didn't have the courage to open myself up to losing someone like that. But being with you, loving you, has made me realize I was wrong."

"How? I'm not courageous," Elana protested.

"You are." Brock tried to make her understand. "After everything you've been through, you opened yourself up to love. With Chloe. With Raine. With Lacey and Tucker." He took a deep breath and let it out slowly. "And I hope with me. Give me a chance, Elana. I love you so much, with my entire heart and soul. Give me a chance to prove how much."

His eyes widened in alarm when her eyes filled with tears. "Brock, I'm the one who should be apologizing to you."

"Why?" He tightened his grip on her hand. Was she trying to tell him she didn't return his feelings?

"You helped me realize that I've been wrong. You asked me to forgive you, and I did. But when you saw my scars, I freaked. Because I hadn't forgiven myself."

"You were young. For heaven's sake, Elana, you had a right to be upset."

"No, you don't understand. I needed to forgive myself for being alive when Felicity wasn't. For loving Chloe while my mother sat day after day in a nursing home. For wishing I could have the family I've always dreamed of."

She paused and then added, "For loving you."

Was she saying what he thought she was saying? "You love me?"

She laughed and threw herself into his arms. He caught her and held her close. "Yes, Brock. I love you. And if you don't want to have a family right away, that's fine with me. Because I love you, and I want you to be happy."

"Elana." He pulled back enough to look into her eyes. "I love you, and I have realized I do want to have a family with you, more than anything else. Will you marry me?"

She smiled, and this time he thought he might be safe in assuming her tears were full of joy. "Yes. I'd be honored to marry you. I love you so much, Brock."

Thank God. He kissed her, knowing that together they could do anything. He held her so tight he didn't ever want to let her go.

"Now my life is complete," he murmured.

EPILOGUE

ELANA stood next to Brock and Joel, the younger brother holding on to a squirmy one-year-old Tucker as Lacey walked across the stage of the technical college auditorium to accept her high school equivalency diploma.

Elana clapped so loudly her hands ached as Brock whistled through his teeth.

"Did you hear Lacey was accepted into college, starting in the fall semester?" Joel said as he helped Tucker wave at his mother as Lacey completed her march across the stage. "She wants to be a teacher."

"I think Lacey will make a great teacher," Elana defended stoutly.

"Me too," Brock added. He glanced down at her, and they exchanged a secret smile. "I heard she got a great scholarship."

"Yeah, she did," Joel said proudly. "All of her tuition is going to be covered, which means we only have to swing the day-care costs. Now that I'm almost finished with my apprenticeship, and will be a full-fledged carpenter, that shouldn't be a problem."

Elana nudged Brock, warning him to keep quiet. She wanted the scholarship to be a surprise. She didn't want Lacey to know where the money came from, at least not until after she was finished with her degree.

Brock lifted her hand and brushed a kiss across her wedding ring. "Your secret is safe with me," he said in a low tone.

"Oh, really?" Elana said, raising a brow. "And what secret is that?"

Brock simply smiled, putting his arm around her and holding her close. Their wedding had been a small affair, held a few months ago, with only their closest friends and family in attendance. She'd been so thrilled her mother had progressed enough to attend. She'd almost wept when her mother had come to wish them well after the ceremony.

She wasn't sure it was fair for one person to be so happy.

As the graduation ceremony drew to a close, they made their way back out of the auditorium to wait for Lacey.

"You don't know all my secrets," Elana said to Brock when Joel and Tucker rushed over to greet Lacey.

"Sure I do."

She slowly shook her head. "I have one big secret." When he rolled his eyes in disbelief, she added, "I'm pregnant."

For a moment he stared at her in shock. "Pregnant? You're pregnant?"

"Do you mind?" Not that she could do much about it now. They'd slipped a few times with using protection, but Brock hadn't seemed too worried. But maybe he wasn't ready for this.

"No! Of course I don't mind. You're having a baby. Our baby!" He swung her up into a bear hug, sweeping her off her feet.

"Shh, this is Lacey's day." She should have waited until later to tell him the news. But his teasing about secrets had made her blurt out the truth.

Now they didn't have any secrets between them.

"Elana, I can't believe it. We're going to have a baby."

"I'm glad you're happy about it; for a minute you had me worried. I love you, Brock." Elana threw her arms around his neck and kissed him. "I'm the luckiest woman in the world."

"I'm the lucky one," he murmured. "Because you've given me my life. A family." He glanced at Joel and Lacey, who were heading towards them, holding Tucker's hands as he walked clumsily on his own two feet between them. "Let's go home."

APRIL 2010 HARDBACK TITLES

ROMANCE

The Italian Duke's Virgin Mistress	Penny Jordan
The Billionaire's Housekeeper Mistress	Emma Darcy
Brooding Billionaire, Impoverished Princess	Robyn Donald
The Greek Tycoon's Achilles Heel	Lucy Gordon
Ruthless Russian, Lost Innocence	Chantelle Shaw
Tamed: The Barbarian King	Jennie Lucas
Master of the Desert	Susan Stephens
Italian Marriage: In Name Only	Kathryn Ross
One-Night Pregnancy	Lindsay Armstrong
Her Secret, His Love-Child	Tina Duncan
Accidentally the Sheikh's Wife	Barbara McMahon
Marrying the Scarred Sheikh	Barbara McMahon
Tough to Tame	Diana Palmer
Her Lone Cowboy	Donna Alward
Millionaire Dad's SOS	Ally Blake
One Small Miracle	Melissa James
Emergency Doctor and Cinderella	Melanie Milburne
City Surgeon, Small Town Miracle	Marion Lennox

HISTORICAL

Practical Widow to Passionate Mistress	Louise Allen
Major Westhaven's Unwilling Ward	Emily Bascom
Her Banished Lord	Carol Townend

MEDICAL™

The Nurse's Brooding Boss	Laura Iding
Bachelor Dad, Girl Next Door	Sharon Archer
A Baby for the Flying Doctor	Lucy Clark
Nurse, Nanny...Bride!	Alison Roberts

0310 Gen Std LP

® MILLS & BOON®

APRIL 2010 LARGE PRINT TITLES

ROMANCE

The Billionaire's Bride of Innocence	Miranda Lee
Dante: Claiming His Secret Love-Child	Sandra Marton
The Sheikh's Impatient Virgin	Kim Lawrence
His Forbidden Passion	Anne Mather
And the Bride Wore Red	Lucy Gordon
Her Desert Dream	Liz Fielding
Their Christmas Family Miracle	Caroline Anderson
Snowbound Bride-to-Be	Cara Colter

HISTORICAL

Compromised Miss	Anne O'Brien
The Wayward Governess	Joanna Fulford
Runaway Lady, Conquering Lord	Carol Townend

MEDICAL™

Italian Doctor, Dream Proposal	Margaret McDonagh
Wanted: A Father for her Twins	Emily Forbes
Bride on the Children's Ward	Lucy Clark
Marriage Reunited: Baby on the Way	Sharon Archer
The Rebel of Penhally Bay	Caroline Anderson
Marrying the Playboy Doctor	Laura Iding

0410 Gen Std HB

ROMANCE

Virgin on Her Wedding Night	Lynne Graham
Blackwolf's Redemption	Sandra Marton
The Shy Bride	Lucy Monroe
Penniless and Purchased	Julia James
Powerful Boss, Prim Miss Jones	Cathy Williams
Forbidden: The Sheikh's Virgin	Trish Morey
Secretary by Day, Mistress by Night	Maggie Cox
Greek Tycoon, Wayward Wife	Sabrina Philips
The French Aristocrat's Baby	Christina Hollis
Majesty, Mistress...Missing Heir	Caitlin Crews
Beauty and the Reclusive Prince	Raye Morgan
Executive: Expecting Tiny Twins	Barbara Hannay
A Wedding at Leopard Tree Lodge	Liz Fielding
Three Times A Bridesmaid...	Nicola Marsh
The No. 1 Sheriff in Texas	Patricia Thayer
The Cattleman, The Baby and Me	Michelle Douglas
The Surgeon's Miracle	Caroline Anderson
Dr Di Angelo's Baby Bombshell	Janice Lynn

HISTORICAL

The Earl's Runaway Bride	Sarah Mallory
The Wayward Debutante	Sarah Elliott
The Laird's Captive Wife	Joanna Fulford

MEDICAL™

Newborn Needs a Dad	Dianne Drake
His Motherless Little Twins	Dianne Drake
Wedding Bells for the Village Nurse	Abigail Gordon
Her Long-Lost Husband	Josie Metcalfe

0410 Gen Std LP

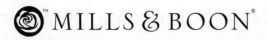

ROMANCE

Ruthless Magnate, Convenient Wife	Lynne Graham
The Prince's Chambermaid	Sharon Kendrick
The Virgin and His Majesty	Robyn Donald
Innocent Secretary...Accidentally Pregnant	Carol Marinelli
The Girl from Honeysuckle Farm	Jessica Steele
One Dance with the Cowboy	Donna Alward
The Daredevil Tycoon	Barbara McMahon
Hired: Sassy Assistant	Nina Harrington

HISTORICAL

Tall, Dark and Disreputable	Deb Marlowe
The Mistress of Hanover Square	Anne Herries
The Accidental Countess	Michelle Willingham

MEDICAL™

Country Midwife, Christmas Bride	Abigail Gordon
Greek Doctor: One Magical Christmas	Meredith Webber
Her Baby Out of the Blue	Alison Roberts
A Doctor, A Nurse: A Christmas Baby	Amy Andrews
Spanish Doctor, Pregnant Midwife	Anne Fraser
Expecting a Christmas Miracle	Laura Iding

millsandboon.co.uk Community

Join Us!

The Community is the perfect place to meet and chat to kindred spirits who love books and reading as much as you do, but it's also the place to:

- **Get the inside scoop from authors about their latest books**
- **Learn how to write a romance book with advice from our editors**
- **Help us to continue publishing the best in women's fiction**
- **Share your thoughts on the books we publish**
- **Befriend other users**

Forums: Interact with each other as well as authors, editors and a whole host of other users worldwide.

Blogs: Every registered community member has their own blog to tell the world what they're up to and what's on their mind.

Book Challenge: We're aiming to read 5,000 books and have joined forces with The Reading Agency in our inaugural Book Challenge.

Profile Page: Showcase yourself and keep a record of your recent community activity.

Social Networking: We've added buttons at the end of every post to share via digg, Facebook, Google, Yahoo, technorati and de.licio.us.

www.millsandboon.co.uk